W9-BPM-465

1.00
Rene

Jacob would make a good father.

That thought sent a shock wave through her. For several seconds she stared at him, then whirled and fled the room. She didn't stop till she was out on the porch. The night air cooled her face.

How could she think something like that? For years she hated Jacob Hartman. In her mind, he wasn't capable of anything good. Now in one day her feelings were shifting, changing into something she didn't want. She felt as though she'd betrayed her family.

Her legs trembling, she plopped down on the front steps. *Lord, I'm a fish out of water. I need the water. I need the familiar. Too much is changing.*

"Hannah, are you all right?" Jacob asked. She hadn't even heard him come out.

"I'm fine," she answered in a voice full of tension. She didn't realize she was holding her breath. He was no fool. He would want to know what was behind her cool reception of him. And she intended to keep her past private.

www.1stChoiceUsedBooks.com

Books by Margaret Daley

Love Inspired

The Power of Love #168
Family for Keeps #183
Sadie's Hero #191
The Courage To Dream #205
What the Heart Knows #236
A Family for Tory #245
*Gold in the Fire #273
*A Mother for Cindy #283
*Light in the Storm #297
The Cinderella Plan #320
*When Dreams Come True #339
*Tidings of Joy #369
**Once Upon a Family #393
**Heart of the Family #425

*The Ladies of Sweetwater Lake
**Fostered by Love

Love Inspired Suspense

Hearts on the Line #23
Heart of the Amazon #37
So Dark the Night #43
Vanished #51
Buried Secrets #72

MARGARET DALEY

feels she has been blessed. She has been married more than thirty years to her husband, Mike, whom she met in college. He is a terrific support and her best friend. They have one son, Shaun.

Margaret has been writing for many years and loves to tell a story. When she was a little girl, she would play with her dolls and make up stories about their lives. Now she writes these stories down. She especially enjoys weaving stories about families and how faith in God can sustain a person when things get tough. When she isn't writing, she is fortunate to be a teacher for students with special needs. Margaret has taught for over twenty years and loves working with her students. She has also been a Special Olympics coach and has participated in many sports with her students.

Heart of the Family
Margaret Daley

Steeple
Hill®

Published by Steeple Hill Books™

If you purchased this book without a cover you should be aware
that this book is stolen property. It was reported as "unsold and
destroyed" to the publisher, and neither the author nor the
publisher has received any payment for this "stripped book."

STEEPLE HILL BOOKS

Steeple
Hill®

ISBN-13: 978-0-373-87461-3
ISBN-10: 0-373-87461-8

HEART OF THE FAMILY

Copyright © 2007 by Margaret Daley

All rights reserved. Except for use in any review, the reproduction
or utilization of this work in whole or in part in any form by any
electronic, mechanical or other means, now known or hereafter
invented, including xerography, photocopying and recording, or in
any information storage or retrieval system, is forbidden without
the written permission of the editorial office, Steeple Hill Books,
233 Broadway, New York, NY 10279 U.S.A.

This is a work of fiction. Names, characters, places and incidents are
either the product of the author's imagination or are used fictitiously, and
any resemblance to actual persons, living or dead, business establishments,
events or locales is entirely coincidental.

This edition published by arrangement with Steeple Hill Books.

® and TM are trademarks of Steeple Hill Books, used under license.
Trademarks indicated with ® are registered in the United States Patent
and Trademark Office, the Canadian Trade Marks Office and in other
countries.

www.SteepleHill.com

Printed in U.S.A.

Then said Jesus, Father, forgive them;
for they know not what they do. And they
parted his raiment and cast lots.

—*Luke* 23:34

To my family: my husband, mother-in-law, son, daughter-in-law and granddaughters

To all the foster parents who have done such a great job helping out in a difficult situation

Chapter One

The child's name on the chart held Jacob Hartman's gaze riveted. Andy Morgan. The eight-year-old from Stone's Refuge had possibly another broken bone. Flashes of the last time the boy had been in his office, only a few weeks before, paraded across his mind.

With a sigh, Jacob entered the room to find the boy perched on the edge of the exam table, his face contorted in pain as he held his left arm, in a makeshift sling, close to his body. A woman Jacob wasn't familiar with stood to the side murmuring soothing words to Andy. She turned toward Jacob, worry etched into her face—and something else he couldn't decipher. Her mouth pinched into a frown that quickly evolved into an unreadable expression.

Jacob shook off the coolness emanating from the young woman. "Hi, Andy. Remember me? I'm Dr. Jacob," he said, using the name the children at the

refuge knew him by. "How did you hurt your arm?"
He gently removed the sling made from an old T-shirt
and took the injured, swollen limb into his hands.

When he probed the forearm, Andy winced and
tried to draw it back. "I fell." The child's lower lip
trembled, and he dug his teeth into it.

"He was climbing the elm tree next to the barn
and fell out of it." When Jacob glanced toward
her, taking in the concern in the woman's dark blue
gaze, she continued in a tense voice that had a soft
Southern lilt. "I'm the new manager at Stone's Refuge. Hannah Smith. I was told when there was a
medical problem to bring the children to you. This
is only my second day, and no one else was around.
The other kids are at school. Andy was supposed to
be there, too. I—" she offered him a brief smile that
didn't reach her eyes "—I talk too much when I'm
upset."

No doubt the tension he felt coming from the
refuge's new manager was due to Andy's accident.
"I take care of the children's medical needs." Jacob
buzzed for his nurse. "Andy, can you do this for
me?" He demonstrated flexing and extending his
wrist and fingers.

With his forehead scrunched, the boy did, but
pain flitted across his features. He tried to mask it,
but Jacob knew what the child was going through.
He'd experienced a few broken bones in his own
childhood and remembered trying to put up a brave
front. He learned to do that well. Jacob unlocked a
cabinet and removed a bottle of ibuprofen.

He handed the boy the pain pills and a glass of water. "Why weren't you at school?" Children like Andy were the reason he had become a pediatrician, but he hadn't quite conquered the feelings generated when he was confronted with child abuse.

The boy dropped his head, cradling his arm against his chest. "I told the other kids I was going back to the cottage because I didn't feel good. I hid instead. I don't like school. I want to go home."

"Just as soon as I get a picture of your arm and we get it fixed up, you can go home."

Andy's head snapped up, his eyes bright. "I can? Really?"

Hannah Smith stepped closer and placed a hand on the child's shoulder. Apprehension marked her stiff actions. "Back home to the refuge."

"No! I want to go *home*." Tears welled up in Andy's brown eyes, and one slid down his thin face.

"Andy, you can't. I'm sorry." Calmness underscored her words as tiny creases lined her forehead. Her concern and caring attitude accentuated her beauty.

Having realized his mistake, Jacob started to respond when the door opened and the nurse appeared. "Teresa, Andy's visiting us again. We need an X-ray of his left arm."

"Hello, Andy. What did you do to your arm?" Teresa, a petite older woman with a huge, reassuring smile, helped the child down from the table. "I bet you remember where our prize box is. Once we get the X-ray done, I'll let you check it out."

"I can?"

"Sure. If I remember correctly, you were also eyeing that red car the last time. It's still there."

"It is?" Andy hurried out of the room, still holding his arm across his chest.

The refuge's manager started to follow the pair. Jacob blocked her path and closed the door. Frowning, she immediately backed up against the exam table.

"I'd like a word with you, Ms. Smith. Teresa will take care of Andy. He knows her. She spent quite a bit of time with him several weeks ago."

Her dark blue gaze fixed on him, narrowing slightly. "I haven't had a chance to read all the children's files yet. What happened the last time he was here?"

Obviously she was upset that something like this occurred on her watch. But beneath her professional demeanor, tension vibrated that Jacob suddenly sensed went beyond what had occurred to Andy. "His mother brought him in with a nasty head wound, and I called social services. Her story didn't check out. Thankfully he was placed quickly at Stone's Refuge."

"I was in the middle of reading the children's files when the school called to find out why he wasn't there. I found Andy lying on the ground hugging his arm and trying his best not to cry, but his face had dry tear marks on it." She pushed her long blond hair behind her ears and blew a breath of air out that lifted her bangs. "When I approached him, he tried to act like nothing was wrong."

"Sadly, Andy is used to holding his pain in. I took several X-rays last time because he was limping and discovered he'd broken his ankle and it was never set properly. He probably will always limp because of the way his bone healed without medical attention."

"His mother didn't seek care for him?"

He shook his head. "I think the only reason she came in last time was because there was so much blood involved. She thought he was dying. He'd passed out briefly. She flew into a rage when he was taken from her." Jacob didn't know if he would ever forget the scene Andy's mother created at the clinic that afternoon. If looks could kill, he would be dead, but then he should be accustomed to that from an angry mother.

"Is there a father?"

"No. I don't think there ever was one in the picture. His mother clammed up and hasn't said anything about the new or old injuries." Jacob picked up the child's chart. "I want you to know what you're dealing with since you haven't been on the job long. The only time Andy cried was when he found out he wasn't going with his mother when he left the hospital. He kept screaming he needed to go home. When he settled down, he whimpered that his mother needed him, but I could never get him to tell me why he thought that." He jotted his preliminary findings down on the chart. "Have you been a social worker for long?"

A gleam glittered in her eyes. "No, I got my degree recently."

A newbie. No wonder she'd wanted to know if Andy's mother had sought help. He would hate to see that light in her eyes dim when the reality of the system sank in. But having dealt with the Department of Human Services and the lack of funding that so often tied its hands when it came to neglected or abused children, he knew the reality of the situation, first as a boy who had gone through the system and now as a pediatrician.

"I've been impressed by the setup at Stone's Refuge, especially since it hasn't been around for long. We could use more places like that." Hannah hiked the straps of her brown leather purse up onto her shoulder. "I'm glad they've started building another house at the ranch. Mr. Stone has quite a vision."

Jacob laughed. "That's Peter. When he came up with using the students from the Cimarron Technology Center to help with the construction of the house, it was a blessing. They're learning a trade, and we're getting another place for kids to stay at a cheaper rate."

"I heard some of his ideas, as well as his wife's when I interviewed with them. It's quite an ambitious project." She started forward. "I'd better check and see—"

The door opened, and Andy came into the room with Teresa and a red car clutched in his hand. "It was there, Dr. Jacob. No one took it."

The child's words, *no one took it,* stirred a memory from Jacob's past. He'd been in his fourth foster home, all of his possessions easily contained in a small backpack. Slowly his treasures had disappeared. The first item had been stolen at the shelter after he'd been removed from his mother's care. By the age of twelve he hadn't expected any of his belongings to stay long, so when he had received a radio for Christmas from a church toy drive, he hadn't thought he would keep it more than a day or so. But when he had moved to his fifth foster home seven months later, he still had the radio in his backpack. No one had taken it. His body had begun to fill out by then, and he'd learned to defend himself with the older children.

"Here's the X-ray, Dr. Hartman."

Teresa handed it to him, drawing him back to the present.

After studying the X-ray, Jacob pointed to an area on Andy's forearm. "That's where it's fractured. Teresa will set you up with Dr. Filmore, an orthopedic surgeon here in the clinic, to take care of your arm."

Andy's eyes grew round. "What will he do?"

"He'll probably put a cast on your arm."

"Can people sign it?" Andy stared at the place where Jacob had pointed on the X-ray.

"Yep, but you won't be able to get it wet. You'll have it on for a few months."

Andy grinned. "You mean, I don't have to take a bath for months?"

Jacob chuckled, ruffling the boy's hair. "I'm afraid a few people might have something to say about that."

"But—"

"We'll rig something up to keep your arm with the cast dry while you take a bath." Hannah moved next to Andy, her nurturing side leaking through her professional facade. "And I'm thinking when we get home, we'll have a cast signing and invite everyone. I've got some neat markers we can use. We can use different colors or just one."

"My favorite color is green."

"Then green it is." Hannah glanced toward Jacob. "Where do we go to see Dr. Filmore?"

Jacob nodded toward Teresa who slipped out of the room. "He's on the third floor. He owes me a favor. If he isn't in surgery, he should be able to see Andy quickly. Teresa will arrange it."

Hannah smiled, her glance straying to Andy. "Great."

It lit her whole face, transforming her plain features into a pretty countenance. It reached deep into her eyes, inviting others to join her in grinning. Jacob responded with his own smile, but when her attention came back to him, her grin died. An invisible but palpable barrier fell into place. Was she still worried about the accident on her second day on the job? Or something else?

As Teresa showed Hannah and Andy out of the room, Jacob watched them leave. He couldn't shake the feeling he'd done something wrong in Hannah's eyes, that her emotional reaction went beyond Andy's accident. Jacob was out at the refuge all the time, since he was the resident doctor for the foster homes and on the board of the foundation that ran Stone's Refuge. But the ice beneath her professional facade didn't bode well for their working relationship. As he headed into the hall, he decided he needed to pay Peter a visit and find out what he could about Hannah Smith.

The sun began its descent toward the line of trees along the side of the road leading to Stone's Refuge. Tension gripped Hannah's neck and shoulders from the hours sitting in the doctor's office, waiting for Andy's arm to be taken care of. No, that wasn't the whole reason. The second she'd seen Dr. Jacob Hartman she'd remembered the time her family had been torn apart because of him. After the death of her older brother, Kevin, everything had changed in her life, and Jacob Hartman had been at the center of the tragedy.

But looking at him, no one could tell what he had done. His bearing gave the impression of a proficient, caring doctor. Concern had lined his face while interacting with Andy. Even now she could picture that look in his chocolate-brown eyes that had warmed when he'd smiled. The two dimples in his cheeks had mocked her when he had turned that grin on her. And for just a second his expression had taunted her to let go of her anger. But she couldn't.

The small boy next to her in the van had been a trouper the whole time, but now he squirmed, his bottled-up energy barely contained. "Mrs. Smith, ya ain't mad at me, are ya?" Andy stared down at his cast, thumping his finger against it over and over.

The rhythmic sound grated on Hannah's raw nerves, but she suppressed her irritation. Andy wasn't the source of her conflicting emotions. "Mad? No. Disappointed, yes. I want you to feel you can come talk to me if something is bothering you rather than playing hooky from school."

Andy dropped his head and mumbled, "Yes, ma'am."

"Please call me Hannah. You and I are the new kids on the block. Actually, you could probably show me the ropes. How long have you been at the house? Two, three weeks?"

He lifted his head and nodded.

"See? This is only my second day. You've got tons more experience at how things are done around here." *Why had she accepted this job? How was she going to work with Dr. Hartman?* The questions screamed for answers she couldn't give.

"Sure. But I don't know too much. The other kids…"

When he didn't continue his sentence, Hannah slanted a look toward him, his chin again resting on his chest, his shoulders curled forward as though trying to draw inward. "What about the other kids?"

"Nothin'."

She slowed the van as she turned onto the gravel road that led to the group of houses for the foster children at Stone's Refuge. "Is anyone bothering you?"

His head came up, and he twisted toward her. "No. It's not that."

In the short time she'd been around the boy, she felt as though she was talking to a child two or three years older, especially now after the half a day spent at the clinic and his staunch, brave face. But after reading part of his file and hearing what the doctor had said, she understood where the boy was coming from. He'd seen the ugly side of life and experienced more than most kids his age. "Then what's wrong?"

"I don't fit in."

Those words, whispered in a raw voice, poked a dagger into old wounds. She had always been the new kid in school. After her family had fallen apart with Kevin's death and her parents divorced, she and her mother had moved around a lot. "Why do you say that?" she managed to get out, although her throat tightened with buried pain she'd thought she had left behind her. But coming back to her hometown where she had lived for the first nine years of her life had been a mistake. How had she thought she wouldn't have to confront what had happened to Kevin? Of course, she hadn't discovered Dr. Jacob Hartman's involvement with the refuge until yesterday.

Andy averted his gaze, hanging his head again. "I just don't. I never have."

The pain produced from his declaration intensified, threatening her next breath. She slowly drew in a lungful of rich oxygen and some of the tension eased. "Then maybe we could work on it together. The staff at the refuge has been there since it opened last year. In fact, I just moved here last week." Cimarron City had been the only place that had resembled a home to her in her wayfaring life. She'd spent much more time here than any other place. Even while attending college, she'd moved several times. She wanted stability and had chosen the familiar town to be where she would put down roots. Maybe that was a mistake.

"You did?"

"Yep." She parked between the two houses she managed—still wanted to manage. This job had been a dream come true—until she realized that Jacob Hartman was involved. "Up until recently, I'd been in school."

"Aren't you too old for that?"

Hannah grinned. "In your eyes, probably. I had to work my way through college as a waitress, which took longer than normal."

Andy tilted his head. "How old are you?"

"Don't you know you aren't supposed to ask a woman how old she is?" she said with a laugh, then immediately added when she saw the distress on his thin face, "But I'll tell you how old if you promise not to tell anyone. I'm twenty-nine."

"Oh," he murmured, as though that age really was ancient.

She almost expected him to say, "I'm sorry," but thankfully he didn't. Instead, he shoved open the door, slowly climbed from the van, and walked toward the house. Seeing him limp renewed her determination to do well in her first professional job, to help these children have a better life.

But she couldn't help thinking: her second day at work and a child in her care had broken a bone. Not good. She would make sure that Andy went to school if she had to escort him every day. She needed to let Laura and Peter Stone, the couple who ran the Henderson Foundation that funded the refuge, know that they were back and what happened with Andy. Hannah looked toward the main house off in the distance, on the other side of the freshly painted red barn.

The refuge was perfect for children who needed someone to care about them. At the moment there were two cottages but the foundation for a third had been poured last week. The best part of the place was the fact it was on a ranch, not far from town. The barn housed abandoned animals that the children helped take care of. The wounded helping the wounded. She liked that idea.

Before she went in search of the couple, she needed to check on Andy and the other seven children in the house where she lived. Meg, her assistant at the cottage and the cook, should be inside since the kids had come home from school an hour ago.

Ten minutes later, after satisfying herself that everything was fine, Hannah trekked across the pasture toward the Stones' place. When she passed in front of the large red double doors thrown open to reveal the stalls inside, she heard a woman's light laugh followed by a deeper one. She changed her direction and entered the coolness of the barn. In the dimness, she saw both Laura and Peter kneeling inside a pen with several puppies roughhousing on the ground in front of them.

"We're going to have a hard time not keeping these." Peter gestured toward the animals that had to be a mix of at least three different breeds.

Laura angled her head toward him. "What's another puppy or two or three when we have so many? They're adorable."

"Are you going blind, woman?"

"Okay, they're so ugly they're cute." Laura caught sight of Hannah and waved her to them. "Don't you think they're cute?"

Hannah inspected the black, brown and white puppies with the elongated squat body of a dachshund, the thick, wiry coat of a poodle and the curly tail and wrinkled forehead of a pug. *Ugly* was an understatement. "I can see their attraction."

Peter's laughter reverberated through the cavernous barn. "I meant that we would have a hard time finding homes for them since they are so— unattractive."

"But that's their appeal. They're different, and you and I love different." Laura stood, dusting off her jean-clad knees.

He swept his arm in a wide arc, indicating the array of animals that had found a refuge at the ranch along with the children. "That's for sure."

Laura stepped over the low pen and approached Hannah. "I heard about Andy. Is he okay?"

"Yes. Broken left forearm. He told me he'd wanted to climb to the very top of that elm tree you have outside the barn."

Laura chuckled. "I've found my twins up there more than once." She glanced back at Peter. "Maybe we should cut it down."

"And rob the kids of a great tree to scale? No way! We'll just have to teach Andy the art of climbing."

"There's an art to climbing trees?" Hannah watched as Peter came up to Laura's side, draped his arm over her shoulder and cradled her against him. Wistfulness blanketed Hannah—a desire to have her own husband and family. She'd almost had that once when she'd married Todd. Would she ever have that kind of love again? A home she would stay in for more than a year?

"Of course. The first rule is to make sure you have good footing before you reach up. I'll talk with Andy."

"He's gonna be in a cast for a few months."

"When he's ready, I'll show him how to do it properly." Peter nuzzled closer to Laura.

"I'm sorry I didn't realize he wasn't on the school bus. If I had, he would—"

Laura shook her head. "Don't, Hannah. Boys will be boys. I have three, and believe me, I know firsthand there's little we can do when they set their minds to do something. I gather you took him to see Jacob."

The name stiffened Hannah's spine. "Yes. He got Andy in to see Dr. Filmore, who put the cast on him."

"We don't know what we would do without Jacob to take care of the children for free." Laura looked up at her husband, love in her eyes. "We've taken up more and more of his time as the refuge has grown."

"Wait until we open the third home. Before we know it, there'll be eight more children for Jacob to take care of." Peter shifted his attention to Hannah. "That should be after the first of the year. Are you going to be ready for the expansion?"

"I'm looking forward to it. The more the merrier." By that time she would know how to deal with Jacob without her stomach tensing into a knot. And hopefully she would become good at masking her aversion because she could do nothing to harm the refuge.

"I knew there was a reason we hired you to run the place. I like that enthusiasm. I've got to check on a mare." Peter kissed his wife's cheek, then headed toward the back door.

"Don't blame yourself for Andy's accident." Laura pinned her with a sharp, assessing regard.

"I'm that obvious?"

"Yep." Laura began walking toward the front of the barn. "Kids do things. They get hurt. Believe me, I know with four children. The twins get into more trouble than five kids. I'm always bandaging a knee, cleaning out a cut."

Outside Hannah saw an old black car coming down the road toward them, dust billowing behind the vehicle. As it neared her, Hannah glimpsed Jacob Hartman driving. Even with him wearing sunglasses, she knew that face. Would never forget that face. She readied herself mentally as the car came to a grinding stop and Jacob climbed from it.

In her last year in college she had discovered the Lord, but she didn't think her budding faith had prepared her to confront the man responsible for her brother's death.

Chapter Two

Jacob's long strides chewed up the distance between him and Hannah. Her heartbeat kicked up a notch. Even inhaling more deep breaths didn't alleviate the constriction in her chest.

A huge grin appeared on his face. He nodded toward Laura, then his warm brown gaze homed in on Hannah. "It's good to see you again. How's Andy doing?"

Lord, help! When she had decided to come back to the town and settle down, she'd discovered Jacob Hartman still lived in Cimarron City and was a doctor, one of nine pediatricians, but why did he have to be involved with *her* children?

"Hannah, are you all right?"

His rich, deep-toned voice penetrated her thoughts. She blinked and focused on his face, his features arranged in a pleasing countenance that made him extra attractive—if she were interested, which she wasn't. His casual air gave the impression of not having a care in the world. Did he even comprehend the pain his actions caused?

"I'm fine." Hannah stuffed her hands into her pants pockets. "Andy's doing okay. He's going around, having everyone sign his cast. If any good has come out of the accident, I would say it has been an icebreaker for him with the others." When she realized she was beginning to ramble, she clamped her lips together, determined not to show how nervous and agitated she was.

Jacob's smile faded as he continued to stare at her. "I'm glad something good came out of it."

Tension invaded his voice, mirroring hers. She curled her hands in her pockets into fists and forced a grin to her lips as she turned toward Laura. "I'd better get back to the house. I just wanted to let you know about Andy. Good day, Dr. Hartman." If she kept things strictly formal and professional, she would be all right.

Hannah started across the pasture toward the refuge, the crisp fall air cooling her heated cheeks. Keep walking. Don't look back. She thought of her Bible in her room at the house and knew she needed to do some reading this evening when the children were settled in their beds. Somehow she had to make enough peace with the situation to allow her to do her job. She wanted what was best for the children and if that meant tolerating Dr. Hartman occasionally, then she could do it. The needs of the children came first.

* * *

"Do you get the feeling that Hannah Smith doesn't like me?" Jacob followed the woman's progress across the field.

Laura peered in the same direction. "There was a certain amount of tension. I just thought it was because of Andy's accident. I think she blames herself."

"I think it's something else." Jacob kneaded the nape of his neck, his muscles coiled in a knot. "Tell me about our new Stone's Refuge's manager."

"She just completed her bachelor's degree in social work from a college in Mississippi."

"What brought her to Oklahoma? The job?"

Laura laughed. "In our short existence we are garnering a good reputation but not that good so we can attract job candidates from out of state. She used to live here once and wanted to come back. She heard about the job from a classmate, who lives in Tulsa, and applied. Personally I think the Lord brought her to us. She's perfect for the job and beat every other candidate hands down."

"High praise coming from you."

"When the third house is finished, we're going to need someone highly organized and capable. We'll have almost thirty children, ranging in ages from five to eighteen. I'm hoping to bring in another couple like Cathy and Roman for the third home and eventually have one in the second cottage, too."

"What happens to Hannah Smith then? I understand she's living in the second cottage right now." He had heard and sensed Hannah's passion for her job earlier and agreed with Laura she would be good as the refuge's manager.

"We'll need someone to oversee all three homes. I can't do it and run the foundation, too. Raising money is a full-time job. If she wants to continue living on-site, we'll come up with something, but I'd like a man and woman in each cottage in the long run, sort of like a surrogate mother and father for the children."

He had pledged himself and his resources to the Henderson Foundation because he knew how lacking good care was for children without a home and family. "I'll do whatever you need."

"I want you to find out what's going on with Hannah. If there's something concerning you, take care of it. She's perfect for the job, and I don't want to lose her. You can charm the spots off a leopard."

"I think you've got me confused with Noah." He peered toward the group homes. "Are you sure there isn't something else I could do?" He wished he had the ease with women that Noah did. His foster brother rarely dated the same lady for more than a month while lately he had no time to date even one woman.

"Yeah, while you're over there, check and see how Andy is faring. I worry about him."

"You worry about all of them."

"Hey, I thought I heard your car." Peter emerged from the barn, a smile of greeting on his face. "What brings you out this way? Is someone sick?"

"Do I have to have a reason to pay good friends a visit?"

Peter slipped his arms around Laura's waist, and she leaned back against him. "No, but I know how busy you've been, and it isn't even flu season yet."

Watching Peter and Laura together produced an ache deep in Jacob's heart. He wanted that with a woman, but Peter was right. His work and church took up so much of his life that he hadn't dated much since setting up his practice two years ago. And you have to date to become involved with a woman, he thought with a wry grin. Maybe Noah could give him lessons after all.

Laura's gaze fastened on him. "Jacob's just leaving. He's going over to check on Andy."

A scowl descended over Peter's features. "Andy's situation is a tough one. His mother is fighting the state. She wants him back."

"To use as a punching bag." Jacob clenched his jaw. He couldn't rid himself of the feeling Andy and his situation were too similar to his own experiences growing up, as though he had to relive his past through the child. He'd been blessed finally to find someone like Paul and Alice Henderson to set him on the right path. "If at all possible, I won't let that happen." He needed to return the gift the Hendersons had given him.

"Stop by and have dinner with us when you're through. I want to discuss the plans for a fourth house."

"Peter, I love your ambition, but the third one

isn't even half-finished." Jacob dug into his pocket for his keys.

"But maybe it will be by the holidays. What a wonderful way to celebrate Christ's birthday with a grand opening!"

"I can't argue with you on that one, but the weather would have to cooperate for that to happen and you know Oklahoma. When has the weather cooperated?" Jacob headed toward his car. He twice attempted to start it before he managed to succeed and pull away from the barn. He had a woman to charm, he thought with a chuckle.

Andy held up his cast. "See all the names I've gotten. All in green."

Hannah inspected it as though it were a work of art. "You even went to the other cottage."

"Yep, I didn't want to leave anyone out."

Because he knew what it was like to be left out, Hannah thought and took the green marker from Andy to pen her own name on the cast. "There's hardly any room left."

He flipped his arm over. "I had them leave a spot for you here."

Hannah wrote her name over the area above his wrist where a person felt for a pulse.

"I've saved a place for Dr. Jacob, too."

Andy's declaration jolted Hannah. She nearly messed up her last letter but managed to save it by drawing a line under her name. "You aren't going back to see Dr. Jacob. Dr. Filmore will be seeing you about your arm." She realized Jacob Hartman was at the barn talking with Peter and Laura, but hopefully he would leave without coming over here. She needed more time to shore up her defenses. The walk across the pasture hadn't been nearly long enough.

"He told me he would come see me. He'll be here. The others said he never breaks a promise."

That was just great! She was considering retreating to her office off her bedroom when the front door opened and the very man she wanted to avoid entered the cottage. His dark gaze immediately sought hers. A trapped sensation held her immobile next to Andy in the middle of the living area off the entrance.

"Dr. Jacob. You came! I knew you would." With his hand cradled next to his chest, Andy hurried across the room and came to an abrupt halt inches from the doctor. The boy grinned from ear to ear. "See all the names I have!" He held up the green marker. "Will you sign it?"

"Where?"

"Right under Hannah's."

"I'd be honored to sign your cast." Jacob again looked at her and said, "I'm in good company," then scribbled his signature on the plaster, a few of his letters touching hers.

The adoring expression on Andy's face galled her. If the boy only knew—Hannah shook that thought from her mind. She would never say anything. She couldn't dwell on the past or she would never be able to deal with Jacob in a civil way. She had to rise above her own anger if she was going to continue to work at Stone's Refuge and put the children's needs before her own.

Was she being tested by God?

She didn't have time to contemplate an answer. Kids flooded into the living room to see Dr. Jacob. In less than five minutes, every child in the house surrounded him, asking him questions, telling him about their day at school.

How had he fooled so many people? Maybe she was here to keep an eye on him. But in her heart she knew that wasn't the reason, because she couldn't see Peter and Laura having anyone but the best taking care of the foster children.

Jacob tousled Gabe's hair. "I see you've got your baseball. How's that throwing arm?"

"Great. You should see me." Gabe grasped Jacob's hand and tugged him toward the front door. "I'll show you."

Jacob allowed himself to be dragged outside, all the kids following. Hannah stepped out onto the porch and observed the impromptu practice in the yard. Laughter floated on the cooling air while the good doctor took turns throwing the ball to various children. They adored Dr. Jacob. She should be cheered by that thought, but Hannah couldn't help the conflicting emotions warring inside her.

If God had put her here to forgive Jacob, she had a long way to go.

"I thought I saw Jacob's car." Cathy, the other

cottage mom, came up next to her at the wooden railing. "It's the ugliest—thing. I can't even call it a car. I sometimes wonder how he even makes it out here in that rolling death trap."

Hannah's fingernails dug into the railing. She hadn't even been able to see Kevin for one last time at his funeral because of how messed up he had been after the car wreck. Although seven of the children were running around and throwing the ball, all she could see was Jacob standing in the middle, smiling, so full of energy and life. Not a care in the world.

Before long several of the boys ganged up on him, and they began wrestling on the ground even though Jacob had on nice khaki pants and a long-sleeved blue cotton shirt. The gleeful sounds emphasized the fun the kids were having. But the scene was tainted by Hannah's perception of Jacob Hartman.

"He's so wonderful with them. If he ever decided to take time for himself, he might find a nice woman to marry and have a boatload of children. He'd make a great dad. Too bad I'm already spoken for."

Seizing the opportunity to turn her back on Jacob, Hannah swung her attention to Cathy. "To a very nice young man."

Her assistant smiled. "I know. Roman is the best husband."

"Where is he?"

"He went over to help Peter at the barn with one of the animals."

"It's nice he works at a veterinarian clinic."

"One day he hopes to go back to school to become a vet even if he's the oldest student in the class."

Hannah relaxed back against the railing, allowing some of the tension to flow from her body. The sounds of continual laughter peppered the air. "I was beginning to think that would be the case with me. It's hard working and going to college at the same time, but it's worth it when you do finally graduate."

"I almost forgot the reason I came out here. I passed through the kitchen and Meg said dinner will be ready in fifteen minutes." Cathy left, walking back to the other cottage next door.

Good. That should put an end to the doctor's visit. Hannah wheeled around and called out to the nearest two girls who were standing off to the side, watching the melee with the boys. "Let's get everyone inside to wash their hands for dinner."

Shortly the group on the ground untangled their limbs and leaped to their feet. They raced toward the door while Jacob moved slowly to rise, his shirttail pulled from his pants, his brown hair lying at odd angles. He tucked in his top and finger combed his short strands.

Andy, who had been standing off to the side watching the fun, shuffled toward Jacob, taking his hand. "Why don't you eat with us, Dr. Jacob?"

The too-handsome man glanced toward her. The child followed the direction of his gaze and asked, "Can he, Hannah?" When she didn't immediately answer, he quickly added, "He'd better check me out before bedtime to make sure I'm okay."

Having stayed behind, too, Gabe took Jacob's other hand. "Yeah. Don't forget you promised me the last time you were here that you'd read a story to me before I went to bed."

That trapped feeling gripped Hannah again. She really didn't have a reason to tell the man no, and yet to spend the whole evening with him wasn't her idea of fun.

Hannah shifted from one foot to the other, realizing everyone was staring at her, waiting for an answer she didn't want to give. She pasted a full-fledged smile on her face that she fought to maintain. "Sure, he can—if he doesn't mind hamburgers, coleslaw and baked beans."

He returned her grin. "Sounds wonderful to a man who doesn't cook. Meg can make anything taste great, even cabbage."

His warm expression, directed totally at her, tempted her cold heart to thaw. "Cabbage is good for you," was all she could think of to say.

"Yeah, I know, but that doesn't mean it tastes good."

"Yuck. I don't like it, either." Gabe puffed out his chest as though he was proud of the fact he and Dr. Jacob were alike in their food preferences.

"Me, neither." Andy followed suit, straightening his thin frame.

Jacob peered down at both boys. "But Meg makes it taste great, and Hannah is right. It's good for you. I'll play a board game with you guys if you finish all your coleslaw. Okay?"

"Yes," the two shouted, then rushed toward the door.

Oh, great. The evening was going to be a long drawn-out affair with games and reading. Maybe she could gracefully escape to her room after dinner while he entertained the children. Hannah waited until he had mounted the porch steps before saying, "Nice recovery."

He gave her another heart-melting grin. "I keep forgetting how impressionable these children can be. They're so hungry for attention and love. I wish I had more time to spend with them."

No! Please don't! She pressed her lips together to keep from saying those words aloud. But she couldn't keep from asking, "Just how involved are you with the refuge?"

He chuckled. "Worried you'll have to be around me a lot?"

Heat scored her cheeks. Obviously she wasn't a very good actress, a fact she already knew. She forced a semi-smile to her lips. "I was curious. I just thought you were the refuge's doctor and that's all."

He planted himself in front of her. "I'm more than that. Peter, Noah and I were the ones who started this. Peter is the one in charge because he lives on the property, but I keep very involved. I'm on the foundation board. This project is important to me."

His words and expression laid down a challenge to her. "It's important to me, too." She took one step back. *He's on the foundation board. It's worse than I thought.*

"Why?"

Although the space between them was a few feet, Hannah suddenly had a hard time thinking clearly. A good half a minute passed before she replied, "I went into social work because I want to make a difference, especially with children who need someone to be their champion. Stone's Refuge gives me a wonderful opportunity to do my heart's desire." *If I can manage my feelings concerning you.*

"Then we have something in common, because that's why I'm involved with the refuge."

The idea they had anything in common stunned Hannah into silence.

The front door opened, and Gabe stuck his head out. "Dr. Jacob, are you coming?"

"Sure. I'll be there in a sec." When the door closed, he turned back to her, intensity in his brown gaze. "I sense we've gotten off on the wrong foot. Somehow we'll have to manage to work together. I won't have the children put in the middle."

She tilted up her chin. "They won't be."

"Good. Then we understand each other."

He left her alone on the porch to gather her frazzled composure. He was absolutely right about never letting the children know how she really felt about their "Dr. Jacob." She had two choices. She could quit the perfect job or she could stay and deal with her feelings about him, come to some kind of resolution concerning Jacob Hartman. Maybe even manage to forgive him.

There really is only one choice.

Trembling with the magnitude of her decision, Hannah sank back against the railing and folded her arms across her chest. She'd never run from a problem in the past, and she wasn't going to now. She didn't quit, either. But most of all, these children needed her. She had so much love to give them. A lifetime of emotions that she'd kept bottled up inside of her while she had been observing life go by her—always an outsider yearning to be included.

So there's no choice. Lord, I need Your help more now than ever before. I want this to work and I can't do it without You. How do I forgive the man who killed my brother because I can't expose his past to the others? The children adore him, and I won't hurt them.

Jacob finished the last bite of his hamburger and wiped his mouth with his napkin. "So next week is fall break. What kind of plans do you all have for the extra two days off from school?"

Several of the children launched into a description of their plans at the same time.

He held up his hand. "One at a time. I think you were first, Gabe."

"Peter wants us to help him when he takes some of the animals to several nursing homes on Thursday."

"And there's a lot of work to be done on the barn expansion." Susie, the oldest child in this cottage, which housed the younger kids, piped up the second Gabe stopped talking.

"He's getting new animals all the time." Terry, a boy with bright red-orange hair, stuffed the last of his burger into his mouth.

Jacob laughed. "True. Word has gotten around about this place."

Nancy nodded. "Yep. I found a kitten the other day in the trash can outside."

Jacob caught Hannah's attention at the other end of the long table. "Do you have any activities planned that you need a chaperone for next week? Maybe I—"

"I think I've got it covered." She looked down at her plate, using her fork to stir the baked beans around in a circle as if it were the most important thing to do.

"I'm sorry, Hannah, I didn't get a chance to tell you I won't be able to go to the zoo with you on Friday." Meg, the cook and helper, stood and removed some of the dishes from the center of the table. "That was the only time I could get in to see the doctor about the arthritis in my knees."

Nancy's blond pigtails bounced as she clapped her hands. "Then Dr. Jacob can go with us!"

Hannah lifted her head and glanced from Meg to Nancy before her regard lit upon him. For a few seconds anxiety clouded her gaze. He started to tell her he didn't have to go when a smile slowly curved her lips, although it never quite touched her eyes.

"You're welcome to come with us to the zoo. It'll be an all-day trip. We leave at ten and probably won't get home until four." Her stare stayed fixed upon him.

The intensity in her look almost made Jacob squirm like Andy, who had a hard time keeping still. She might not have meant it, but deep in her eyes he saw a challenge. Determined to break down the barrier she'd erected between them, he nodded. "I'll be here bright and early next Friday, and I even know how to drive the minibus."

"That's great, since I don't think Hannah's had a chance to learn yet. If you aren't used to it, it can be a bit awkward." Meg stacked several more plates, then headed for the kitchen.

"You can take that kind of time off just like that?" Hannah snapped her fingers.

"I always leave some time during a break or the holidays for the kids."

"Yep." Terry, the child who had been at the cottage the longest, stood to help Meg take the dishes into the kitchen.

"Well, then it's settled. I appreciate the help, especially with the minibus." Hannah rose. "Who has homework still to do tonight?" She scanned the faces of the eight children at the dining-room table.

Several of them confessed to having to do more homework and left to get their books.

Gabe, short for his nine years, held up his empty plate. "I ate all my coleslaw."

"Me, too." Andy gestured toward his as Susie took it.

"You two aren't part of the cleanup crew?" Jacob gave the girl his dishes.

Both boys shook their heads.

"Then get a game out, and I'll be in there in a minute."

"Can I play, too?" Nancy leaped to her feet. "I don't have to clean up."

Gabe frowned and started to say something, but Jacob cut him off with, "Sure you can."

Nancy, being in kindergarten, was the youngest in the house. Jacob suspected that and the fact she was a girl didn't set well with Gabe, and judging by Andy's pout, him, either. But Jacob knew the importance of bonding as a family and that meant every child, regardless of sex or age, should have an opportunity to play.

Gabe and Andy stomped off with Nancy right behind them, her pigtails swinging as she hurried to keep up. Jacob turned toward Hannah and noticed the dining-room table had been cleared and they were totally alone now. That fact registered on her face at the same time. Her eyes flared for a second, then an indecipherable expression descended as though a door had been shut on him.

"I'm glad we have a few minutes alone." The look of surprise that flashed into her eyes made him smile. "I forgot to tell you earlier that Andy's mother is fighting to get him back. Peter just found out today."

"She is?"

"And I'm not going to let that happen. I've seen his injuries." *I've been there. I know the horror.* "He's better off without her."

"If she cleans up her act and stops taking drugs,

he might be all right going back home. In the short time I've been around him, I've seen how determined he is to get back there."

"He isn't better off if he returns to her. Believe me."

A puzzled look creased her forehead. "Then why does he want to go home?"

He shook his head slowly. "You're new at this. Take my word in this situation—he shouldn't go back to his mother. He's the caretaker in that family of two and he feels responsibility as a parent would. Certainly his mother doesn't."

Hannah's face reddened. She came around the side of the table within a few feet of him. "How do you know this for a fact? Has Andy said anything to you?"

"No, I just know. I was in foster care for many years. I've seen and heard many things you've never dreamed of. Give yourself a year. Your attitude that the birth parent is best will change."

"I believe if it's possible a family should be together. Tearing one apart can be devastating to a child."

The ardent tone in her voice prodded his anger. His past dangled before him in all its pain and anguish. His heartbeat thundered in his ears, momentarily drowning out the sounds of the children in the other room. "Keeping a family together sometimes can be just as devastating." He balled his hands at his sides. "Why did you really go into social work?" he asked as though her earlier reason wasn't enough.

Her own temper blazed, if the narrowing of her eyes was any indication. "As I told you earlier, to help repair damaged families. But if that isn't possible, to make sure the children involved are put in the best situation possible."

His anger, fed by his memories, sizzled. Before he said anything else to make their relationship even rockier, he spun around and left her standing in the dining room.

The children's laughter, coming from the common living area, drew him. He needed that. For years he'd dealt successfully with the wounds of his childhood by suppressing them. Why were they coming to the surface now?

Lord, what are You trying to tell me? Aren't I doing enough to make up for what I did? What do You want of me?

Jacob stepped into the room and immediately Gabe and Andy surrounded him and pulled him toward the table in front of the bay window where the game was set up. Nancy sat primly, toying with a yellow game piece. Her huge grin wiped the past few minutes from his mind as he took his chair between the boys.

He lost himself in the fun and laughter as the three kids came gunning for him. He kept being sent back to the start and loving every second of it. Until he felt someone watching him. Jacob glanced up and found Hannah in the doorway, a question in her eyes—as though she couldn't believe a grown man was having so much fun playing a kid's game. He certainly hadn't done much of this as a child.

Across the expanse of the living room that challenge he had sensed earlier reared up. If she was staying at the refuge as its manager, then he would have to find a way for this situation to work. He didn't want the kids to feel any animosity between him and Hannah. They'd had enough of that in their short lives. Before he left tonight, he would find out exactly why she was wary of him.

Chapter Three

Hannah stood in the entrance into the living room and observed the children interacting with Jacob. She hadn't intended to stay and watch them play, but for some reason she couldn't walk away. Jacob had a way with the kids, as if he knew exactly where they were coming from and could relate to them on a level she didn't know she would ever reach.

The bottom line: he was good with them. Very good.

When the trip to the zoo had come up at dinner, she hadn't wanted Jacob to come. Now though, she saw the value in him being a part of the outing.

A fact: if she stayed, Jacob would be in her life whether she wanted him to or not. She was a realist, if nothing else, and she would come to terms with her feelings concerning him for the children's sake.

Andy yawned and tried to cover it up with his palm over his mouth. When he dropped his hand away, however, his face radiated with a smile as Jacob directed a comment to him.

"Gotcha! Sorry but you've got to go back to the start, buddy." Jacob triumphantly removed Andy's peg from its slot and put it at the beginning.

Gabe took his turn and brought one of his pieces home. He pumped the air and shouted his glee. "I've only got one more out. I'm gonna win!"

Hannah needed to check to see if the others were doing their homework. But she found she couldn't leave. There was something about Jacob that kept her watching—after years of hating the man for what he'd done to her family.

At Gabe's next turn he jumped up and pranced about in a victory dance as if he'd crossed the goal line. "I finally won!"

Andy tried to grin but couldn't manage it. Instead he blinked his eyes open wide and yawned again—and again.

Hannah entered the room. "Gabe, please put the game up. It's time for bed."

"But we haven't played enough." Gabe stopped, a pout pushing his lips out.

Jacob began removing the pegs from the board. "You'd better do as she says or I might not get to read you a story. If there's not enough—"

Gabe leaped toward the table and scrambled to put up the game. Andy's head nodded forward. Nancy stifled her own yawn.

Hannah made her way to Andy's side and knelt next to him. "Time for bed."

His head snapped up, his eyes round as saucers. "No. No, another game. I haven't won yet."

"Sorry. You'll have to wait for another day." Hannah straightened.

"Andy, I'll make you a promise, and you know I don't go back on them. The next time I'm here, we'll play any game you want." Jacob stood and moved to the boy, saying to Hannah, "Here, I'll take him to his room," then to Andy, "I think everything has finally caught up with you, buddy. You've been great! I can't believe you went this long. Most kids would have been asleep hours ago after the day you had."

As Jacob scooped up the eight-year-old into his arms and headed to the boys' side of the house, Andy beamed up at him, then rested his head on Jacob's shoulder.

After hurriedly putting the game away, Gabe raced to catch up with them. "We share a room."

Nancy looked sleepily up at Hannah. "I want a story, too."

"How about if I read one to you? You get ready for bed while I check on the others finishing their homework."

Nancy plodded toward the girls' side while Hannah went back into the dining room where Terry and Susie were the only ones still doing their work. "How's it coming?"

Susie looked up, a seriousness in her green eyes. "We're almost done."

"Need any help?"

"Nope." After scratching his fingers through his red hair, Terry erased an answer to a math problem on his paper. "Susie had this last year in school. She's been helping me."

Leaving the two oldest children, Hannah walked to Nancy's room and found the little girl in her pajamas, stretched out asleep on her twin bed's pink coverlet. Her clothes were in a pile on the floor beside her. Her roommate was tucked under her sheets, sleeping, too. Hannah gently pulled the comforter from under Nancy and covered her, then picked up the child's clothes and placed them on a chair nearby.

With the youngest girls in bed, Hannah made her way to the boys' side to see how Gabe and Andy were doing. The evening before, her first night in the cottage, both of them had been a handful to get to bed. Even with Andy half asleep, Jacob could be having trouble.

Sure, Hannah, she asked herself, *is that the real reason you're checking on them?*

At the doorway she came to a halt, her mouth nearly dropping open at the scene before her. Andy was in bed, lying on his side, desperately trying to keep his eyes open as he listened to the story Jacob was reading. The doctor lounged back against Gabe's headboard with the boy beside him, holding the book on his lap and flipping the pages when Jacob was ready to go on to the next one. Neither child was bouncing off the walls. Neither child was whining about going to bed. Jacob's voice was calm and soothing, capable of lulling them to sleep with just the sound of it.

Cathy is right. Jacob would make a good father.

That thought sent a shock wave through her. She took a step back at the same time Jacob peered up at her, the warmth in his gaze holding her frozen in place. For several seconds she stared at him, then whirled and fled the room. She didn't stop until she was out on the porch. The night air cooled her face, but it did nothing for the raging emotions churning her stomach.

How could she think something like that? For years she had hated Jacob Hartman. In her mind he wasn't capable of anything good. Now in one day her feelings were shifting, changing into something she didn't want. She felt as though she had betrayed her family, the memory of her brother.

Her legs trembling, she plopped down on the front steps and rubbed her hands over her face. *Lord, I'm a fish out of water. I need the water. I need the familiar. Too much is changing. Too fast.*

She leaned back, her elbows on the wooden planks of the porch, and stared up at the half-moon. Stars studded the blackness. No clouds hid the beauty of a clear night sky. The scent of rich earth laced the breeze. Everything exuded tranquility—except for her tightly coiled muscles and nerves shredded into hundreds of pieces.

She'd lived a good part of her life dealing with one change after another—one move after another, the accidental death of her husband after only one year of marriage. She had come to Cimarron City finally to put down roots and hopefully to have some permanence in her life. *Instead I'm discovering more change, more disruption.*

"Hannah, are you all right?"

She gasped and rotated toward Jacob who stood behind her. So lost in thought, she hadn't even heard him come out onto the porch. She didn't like what the man was doing to her. She wanted stability—finally.

"I'm fine," she answered in a voice full of tension.

He folded his long length onto the step next to her. She scooted to the far side to give him room and her some space. His nearness threatened her composure. Leaning forward, he placed his elbows on his thighs and loosely clasped his hands together while he studied the same night sky as she had only a moment before. His nonchalant poise grated along her nerves, while inside she was wound so tightly she felt she'd break any second.

She didn't realize she was holding her breath until her lungs burned. She drew in deep gulps of air, suffused with the smells of fall, while grasping the post next to her, all the strain she was experiencing directed toward her fingers clutching the poor piece of wood.

He was no fool. He would want to know what was behind her cool reception of him. And she intended to keep her past private. After today she knew now more than ever the secret could harm innocent people—children. She couldn't do that for a moment of revenge. Their shared past would remain a secret.

"Have we met before this morning?" he asked, finally breaking the uncomfortable silence.

She sighed. This was a question she could answer without lying. "No." She was relieved that her last name was no longer the same as her brother's.

"I thought maybe we had, and I'd done something you didn't like."

"I've never met you before this morning." Which was true. Kevin and Jacob hadn't been friends long when the car wreck occurred. She felt as though she were running across a field strewn with land mines and any second she would step in the wrong spot.

"I get the feeling you don't care for…my involvement in the refuge."

Thank You, Lord. His choice of words made it possible for her not to reveal anything she didn't want to. "I've seen how you interact with the kids this evening. They care very much for you. How could I not want that for them? They don't have enough people in their lives who do."

Jacob faced her. "Good. Because I intend to continue being involved with them, and I didn't want there to be bad feelings between us. The children can sense that. Gabe already said something right before he went to sleep."

"He did? What?"

Although light shone from the two front windows, shadows concealed his expression. "He wanted to know what we had fought about. He thought I might have gotten mad at you because Andy got hurt. I assured him that accidents happen, and I wasn't upset with you."

Hannah shoved to her feet. "I should go say something to him."

"What?"

"Well…" She let her voice trail off into the silence while she frantically searched for something ambiguous. "I need to assure him, too, that we haven't fought."

"By the time I left him he was sound asleep. I've never seen a kid go to sleep so fast. I wish I had that ability."

Had he ever lost sleep over what he did, as she had? "You have a lot of restless nights?" slipped out before she could censor her words.

He surged to his feet, and his face came into view. "I have my share."

The expression in his eyes—intense, assessing— bored into her. She looked away. "It's been a long second day. I need to make sure the rest of the children go to bed since they have school tomorrow. Good night."

She'd reached the front door when she heard him say in a husky voice, "I look forward to getting to know you. Good night, Hannah."

Inside she collapsed back against the wooden door, her body shaking from the promise in his words. Against everything she had felt over twenty-one years, there was a small part of her that wanted to get to know him. His natural ability to connect with these children was a gift. She could learn from him.

On the grounds at the Cimarron City Zoo Hannah spread the blanket out under the cool shade of an oak tree, its leaves still clinging to its branches. Not a cloud in the sky and the unusually hot autumn day made it necessary to seek shelter from the sun's rays. She'd already noticed some red-tinged cheeks, in spite of using sunscreen on the children. Susie, the last one in Hannah's group to get her food from the concession stand, plopped down on the girls' blanket a few feet from Hannah's.

Where were the boys and Jacob? She craned her neck to see over the ridge and glimpsed them trudging toward her. Jacob waved and smiled.

Terry hurried forward. "I got to see a baby giraffe! Giraffes are my favorite animal."

"I'm not sure I can pick just one favorite." Out of the corner of her eye she followed Jacob's progress toward her. He spoke to the guys around him, and they all headed toward the concession stand. "You'd better go get what you want for lunch." Hannah nodded toward the departing boys and Jacob.

Terry whirled around and raced after them. Ten minutes later everyone was settled on the blankets and stuffing hamburgers or hot dogs into their mouths.

Nibbling on a French fry, Hannah thought of the trip this morning to the zoo on the other side of Cimarron City with Jacob driving. Not too bad.

She'd managed to get a lively discussion going about what animals they were looking forward to seeing.

Quite a few of the children had never been to a zoo and were so excited they had hardly been able to sit still in the minibus. Andy literally bounced around as though trying to break the restraints of the seat belt about him. Since his accident he had gone to school every day and the minute he returned to the cottage he would head to the barn to help with the animals. Last night he had declared to her at dinner that he wanted to be a vet and that he was going to help Peter and Roman with "his pets."

"May I join you?"

Jacob's question again took her by surprise. She swung her attention to him standing at her side. She glanced toward the other two blankets and saw they were filled with the children. "Sure." She scooted to the far edge, giving the man as much room as possible on the suddenly small piece of material.

"How are things going so far?" Jacob sat, stretching one long leg out in front of him and tearing open his bag of food, then using his sack as a large platter.

"Good. The girls especially liked the penguins and the flamingos."

"Want to guess where we stayed the longest?" Jacob unwrapped his burger and took a bite.

"The elephants?"

"Haven't gone there yet."

"We haven't, either."

"Why don't we go together after lunch? They have a show at one."

"Fine." Her acceptance came easier to her lips than she expected. He'd been great on the ride to the zoo. He'd gotten the kids singing songs and playing games when the discussion about animals had died down. Before she had realized it, they had arrived, and she had been amazed that the thirty-minute trip she had dreaded had actually been quite fun. "So where did y'all stay the longest?"

"At the polar bear and alligator exhibits. Do you think that means something? The girls like birds and the boys like ferocious beasts?"

Her stomach flip-flopped at the wink he gave her. Shock jarred her. Where had that reaction come from? "I had a girl or two who liked the polar bears. One wanted a polar bear stuffed animal."

"Let me guess. Susie?"

She shook her head. "Nancy."

He chuckled. "I'm surprised. She's always so meek and shy."

"She's starting to settle in better." Nancy had only been at the refuge two weeks longer than Andy, and being the youngest at the age of five had made her adjustment to her new situation doubly hard on her.

"That's good to hear," he said in a low voice. "Her previous life had been much like Andy's, except that her mother doesn't want her back. I heard from Peter this morning that she left town."

Hannah's heart twisted into a knot. How could a mother abandon her child? Even with all that had happened in her life, she and her mother had stuck together. "I always have hope that the parents and children can get back together."

Jacob's jaw clamped into a hard line. He remained quiet and ate some of his hamburger. Waves of tension flowed off him and aroused her curiosity. Remembering back to her second night at the cottage, she thought about his comments concerning Andy and his mother fighting to get him back. What happened to Jacob to make him feel so fervent about that issue? Was it simply him being involved with the refuge or something more personal? *And why do I care?*

For some strange reason the silence between her and Jacob caused her to want to defend her position. She lowered her voice so the children around them wouldn't overhear and said, "I was up a good part of the night with Nancy. I ended up in the living room, rocking her while she cried for her mother. It tore my heart to listen to her sorrow, and I couldn't do anything about it."

"Yes, you did. You comforted her. Her mother wouldn't have. She left her alone for days to fend for herself."

"But her mother was who she wanted."

"Because she didn't know anyone else better."

The fierce quiet of his words emphasized what wasn't being spoken. That this conversation wasn't just about Nancy. "But if we could work with parents, give them the necessary skills they need to cope, teach them to be better parents—"

"Some things can't be taught to people who don't want to learn."

"Children like Nancy and Andy, who are so young and want their mothers… I think we have to try at least."

"Andy wants to go home. He never said he wanted his mother. There's a difference."

Hannah clutched her drink, relishing the coldness of the liquid while inside she felt the fervor of her temper rising. "Maybe not in Andy's mind. Just because he doesn't say he wants his mother doesn't mean he doesn't. The biological bond is a strong one."

"Hannah, can we play over there?" Susie pointed to a playground nearby with a place to climb on as though a large spider had spun a web of rope.

All the children had finished eating while she and Jacob had been arguing and hadn't eaten a bite. A couple of the boys gathered the trash and took it to the garbage can while Terry and Nancy folded the blankets. "Sure. We'll be done in a few minutes."

"Take your time." Susie raced toward the play area with several of the girls hurrying after her.

When the kids had cleared out, Hannah turned back to Jacob to end their conversation, since she didn't think they would ever see eye to eye on the subject, and found him staring at her. All words fled her mind.

One corner of his mouth quirked. "Do you think she heard?"

Granted their words had been heated, but Hannah had made sure to keep her voice down. "No, but I'm glad they're playing over there." She gestured toward the area where all the children were now climbing on the spiderweb, leaping from post to post or running around. "While in college I helped out at a place that worked to find foster homes for children in the neighborhood where their parents lived."

"I'm sure that was a complete success." Sarcasm dripped over every word.

"Actually they had some successes and some failures, but those successes were wonderful. They went beyond just placing the children near their parents. They counseled the parents and tried to get help for them. While I was there, several made it through drug rehab and were becoming involved in their child's life again. The children still stayed in their foster home while the problems were dealt with, but the kids didn't feel abandoned by their parents. That went a long way with building up their self-esteem."

"What about the child's safety and welfare when that parent backslides and starts taking drugs or abusing alcohol again?" Jacob pushed to his feet and hovered over her.

His towering presence sent her heart hammering. She rose. "You can't dismiss the importance of family ties."

He glared at her. "I've seen too many cases where family ties meant nothing."

She swung her attention to the children playing five yards away, but she sensed his gaze on her, drilling into her. "Family is everything."

"I'm not saying family isn't important—when it is the right one. When it isn't, it destroys and harms a child."

She noticed Andy say something to a woman. "I can understand where you're coming—"

"Don't!"

Out of the corner of her eye she saw Jacob pick up the blanket they'd been on and begin folding it. When she looked back to the children, she counted each one to make sure everyone was there. Shoulders hunched, Andy, now alone, sat on a post and watched the others running around and climbing on the ropes.

Jacob came up to her side. "I was in foster care. I got over it and moved on."

"So these children will, too?"

"With our help."

Andy walked a few feet toward her and stopped. "Hannah, I'm going to the restroom."

"Sure, it's right inside the concession stand." She started toward the boy.

Andy tensed. "I can go by myself. I'm eight!"

"I'll just be out here on the porch waiting for you, then we're going to the elephant exhibit."

He grinned. "Great."

Five minutes later Jacob rounded up the children on the playground when Andy came out of the concession stand.

"I can't wait to see the elephants." The boy limped toward the large group heading toward the other side of the zoo.

Hannah took up the rear as they made their way to the elephant building. Inside, the kids dispersed to several different areas. Andy and Gabe crowded around the skeleton with another group. People packed the Elephant Enclosure with a few youngsters running around, shouting.

Jacob stared toward the entrance, a frown descending.

"What's wrong?"

He shook his head as though to clear it. "I thought I saw someone—" he scanned the area "—but I guess I didn't."

"Who?"

"Andy's mother."

Alarm slammed Hannah's heartbeat against her rib cage. "Let's get our children together." She began gathering the girls into the center of the exhibit.

One pair of boys joined the four girls. Hannah counted six. She searched for Jacob, Gabe and Andy. She found Jacob with Gabe off to the side of the skeleton. The fear and concern in the man's expression told Hannah something was wrong—very wrong. She corralled the kids near her and hurried toward the two.

"Where's Andy?"

Tears streaked down Gabe's face. "Andy told me to be quiet. Then he left with a lady."

Jacob leaned close to her and whispered, "It *was* his mother I saw. She has him."

Chapter Four

The fury in Jacob's words scorched Hannah. She stepped back and scanned the throng at the zoo, checking the exits. All the children were watching her. She schooled her expression into a calm one. When she faced Jacob again, his jaw clenched into an impenetrable line.

"I'll notify security. Keep the kids together." He didn't give Hannah a chance to say anything. He strode toward a man wearing a zoo uniform.

"Hannah, will Andy be all right?" Terry stood in front of the children as if he were their spokesman.

"He isn't with a stranger. He's with his mother. He'll be fine." She prayed she was right. "There's nothing to worry about. Let's go outside where it's less crowded." She took Nancy's and Gabe's hand and headed for the door nearest them.

As she left the building, she caught Jacob's attention and pointed toward the exit. The grim look on his face didn't bode well. *Lord, please bring Andy back to us safe and sound.*

Hannah sought a shaded area where she could keep an eye on the door into the Elephant Enclosure. The children circled her with Gabe off to the side. Tears ran down his cheeks. She drew him to her and draped her arm over his shoulder.

"I didn't...mean—" Gabe released a long sob "—to do anything wrong."

"Sometimes keeping a secret isn't a good thing."

Gabe looked up at her, fear invading his blurry gaze. "Am I in trouble?"

Hannah gave the boy a smile. "No." Then she surveyed the other six children and added, "But this is a good time to talk about what y'all should do if someone approaches you and wants you to go with them. Don't go without first checking with one of the staff at the refuge. Even if you know that person." She made eye contact with each child.

Susie broke from the circle and hurried past Hannah. "Dr. Jacob, did you find Andy?"

Hannah pivoted and saw relief in Jacob's expression as he nodded. The tautness in her stomach uncoiled. "Where is he?"

"Security has him and his mother at the front gate. I told them we'd be right there."

Hannah gathered the children into a tight group, then they headed toward the zoo entrance. A member of security waited in front of a building. The young man indicated a door for them to go through.

Inside Andy sat in a chair with another security guard at a desk.

Hannah hurried to Andy and sat in the vacant seat beside him while the other children milled about the room, trying not to look at them. "Are you all right?"

Swinging his legs, Andy stared at his hands entwined together in his lap and mumbled, "Where's my mom?"

Hannah scanned the area and noticed Jacob talking with a man who appeared to be in charge. "I don't know."

He lifted his tear-streaked face. "They took her away."

"Who?"

Andy pointed toward the guard nearest him, his hand shaking. "One of them."

Hannah patted his knee. "Let me find out what's going on. Stay right here."

His head and shoulders sagged forward. "I want to see my mom." He sniffed. "She came to see me."

The quaver in the child's voice rattled Hannah's composure. All she wanted to do was draw him into her arms and hold him until the hurt went away. Instead she rose and crossed the room to Jacob and the security guard by the desk.

Susie approached. "Is Andy all right? Can we help?"

"He'll be fine. And if you can keep the others quiet and together over there—" she waved her hand toward an area off to the side "—that would be great."

"Sure. I'll get Terry to help me." The young girl hurried to her friend and whispered into his ear.

As Susie and Terry gathered the children into a group and lined them up along the wall, Hannah stopped near Jacob by the desk. "Where's Andy's mother?"

"Security has called the police for me. They're on their way. She violated a court order. She can't see Andy unless it's a supervised visit arranged ahead of time."

Hannah glanced over her shoulder to make sure Andy—for that matter, the other children, too—hadn't heard what Jacob said. Thankfully he'd kept his voice low. The boy continued to look down at his hands. "Andy wants to see her."

"No!"

Although whispered, the force behind that one word underscored Jacob's anger. From the few comments he'd made, Hannah wondered what was really behind his fury. She moved nearer in order to keep their conversation private, aware of so many eyes on them. "She's still his mother. We could be in the room with them to make sure everything is all right."

He thrust his face close. "I won't have that woman disrupt his life any more than she already has by pulling this stunt."

She met his glare with her own. "I am the manager at the refuge, and I do have a say in what is done with the children."

Jacob started to speak but instead snapped his jaw closed.

"I'll talk with Andy's mother first and see what prompted this action today."

"It won't do any good. She doesn't deserve a child like Andy."

There were so many things she wanted to retort, but she bit the inside of her mouth to keep her thoughts quiet. It was important that Andy not realize they were arguing over him. "Beyond that day in your office, have you had any contact with the woman?"

His eyes narrowed. "No."

"Then let me assess the situation." Again she sent a quick glance toward Andy then the other seven kids to make sure they weren't hearing what was said. "If I don't think her intentions are honorable, I won't let her see Andy. Deal?" She presented her hand to seal the agreement.

Jacob looked at it then up into her face. His fingers closed around hers, warm, strong. "Deal. But I want you to know I don't think this is a good idea."

She wasn't sure it was, either, but for Andy's sake, she needed to try. Maybe there was a way to salvage their family if the mother was trying this hard to see her son.

"Where's Andy's mother?" she asked the head of security, not sure that Jacob would have told her.

The man pointed toward a door at the end of the hall where another guard stood. She made her way down the short corridor, stopping for a moment in front of Andy to give him a reassuring smile. His tear-filled eyes reinforced her resolve to try and make this work for him.

At the door she paused and peered back. Jacob's sharp gaze and the tightening about his mouth emphasized his displeasure at what she was attempting. Then she swung her attention to Andy, and the hopefulness she saw in his expression prodded her forward.

Lord, let this work. Help me to reach Andy's mother somehow.

When Hannah entered the room, she found Andy's mom sitting at a table, her head down on it as though she was taking a nap. The sound of the door closing brought the woman up, her gaze stabbing Hannah with fury.

"You don't have no right to take my son away. I wanna see Andy."

Calmness flowed through Hannah. She moved to the table and took the chair across from Andy's mother. "I'm Hannah Smith, the manager at Stone's Refuge where your son is staying." She held her hand out.

The young woman glared at it, then angled sideways to stare at the wall.

"Mrs. Morgan, Andy wants to see you, but I want to be assured that you won't upset him and cause a scene."

Again her angry gaze sliced to Hannah. "He should be with me. This ain't none of your business. He's my son!"

Hannah assessed the woman, focusing on her eyes to try and discern if she was on any drugs. Other than anger, she didn't see anything that indicated she was high. "The court has taken Andy away from you and is reviewing your parental rights. You may see Andy when you make prior arrangements with his case manager. You can't see him alone."

Some of the anger leaked from her expression. "I just wanna see my baby. I shouldn't have to ask for permission. I haven't taken no drugs in days."

"That's good. Would you consider going into a rehab facility?"

Her teeth chewed on her lower lip. "Yes. Anything. Will I get Andy back then?"

"That isn't my decision. It will have to be the court's. But it will be a step in the right direction." Hannah folded her hands on the table, lacing her fingers together. "How did Andy get hurt the last time you were with him?"

Tears sprang into the young woman's eyes. "It was an accident. He fell and hit his head." Her gaze slid away from Hannah.

"Why did he fall?"

Silence. Andy's mother bit down hard on her lip.

"If I'm going to help you, I need to know everything. I need the truth."

The young woman opened her mouth to speak, but clamped it closed without saying anything. The indentation in her lower lip riveted Hannah's attention. When she finally peered into Andy's mother's eyes, a tear rolled down her cheek.

"If you're serious about being in Andy's life, you have to trust me."

The lip with the teeth marks quivered. "My boyfriend pushed him away." More tears welled into Andy's mother's eyes and fell onto the table.

"Why did he do that?"

Mrs. Morgan dropped her head, much as Andy often did. "Because he was hitting me and Andy wanted to stop him."

"I see."

Her head jerked up. "No, ya don't! He didn't want me to take him to the doctor. Andy was throwing up. When my boyfriend passed out, I brought my baby to see Dr. Hartman. That's when everything went bad. They took Andy from me. I went home and my boyfriend had left me. He's—he's— I'm all alone." She swiped her trembling hands across her cheeks. "I don't—" she sucked in a shuddering breath "—wanna be alone."

"So all Andy's injuries were caused by this boyfriend?"

"Yes, yes, I'd never hurt my baby. Never!" Tears continued to flow from her eyes.

"But staying with your boyfriend did hurt your child."

"I know, but I don't have no money. I'm—" Andy's mother sagged forward and cried. "I love Andy. I..." The rest of the words were lost in the woman's sobs.

Hannah came around the table and touched her shaking shoulder. "Let's start with you talking to Andy. If that goes well, we can discuss the next step, Mrs. Morgan."

The woman lifted her head, rubbing her hands

down her face. "My name is Lisa Morgan. I ain't never been married."

"How old are you?" Hannah went back to her chair.

"Twenty-three. I can't pay for rehab. I don't have no money." She dashed her hands across her cheeks then through her hair.

"Let me worry about that. When you think you're ready, I'll go get Andy."

Lisa straightened, smoothing her shirt. "I'm ready to see my baby."

Hannah pushed to her feet and headed for the door. She hoped she was doing the right thing, that Jacob was wrong. Lisa had been a child when she'd had Andy. Maybe she'd never had a break.

Out in the hall she motioned for Andy to come to her. She caught Jacob's regard over the heads of all the kids who had surrounded him in the security office. "We won't be long. Maybe the children would like to ride the train."

"Yeah!" several of them shouted.

"Can we?" Terry asked Jacob.

"Sure."

His gaze intent on her, Jacob crossed to her while she opened the door into the small room where Lisa was. Andy slipped inside. Out of the corner of her eyes, she saw the boy throw himself into his mother's outstretched arms and plaster himself against her. His cries mingling with his mother's could be heard in the hallway.

"This is a mistake," Jacob whispered while he peered inside at Andy and his mom.

"What if it isn't?" Hannah lifted her chin a notch. "I'm going to have security call the police back and tell them they don't have to come."

"She should be held accountable for breaking the court order." A steel thread weaved through each word.

"That will only happen if, as a member of the foundation board, you overrule me." She directed a piercing look at him. "Are you?"

He met her glare for glare while a war of emotions flitted across his face. Finally resignation won. "No, I'm not going to. But don't leave them alone together." He pivoted and strode to the group of children hovering around the head of security's desk, asking him tons of questions.

Hannah paused in the entrance into the room and said to the guard nearby, "Please call the police and tell them it isn't necessary to come." Then she went in and closed the door.

"Mom, when can I come home?" Andy pulled back from his mother. "I miss ya."

Lisa shifted in the chair until she faced her son, clasping his hands. "And I missed ya, too. I have some things to work out, but once I do, you'll be able to come home with me."

"When?"

Lisa shook her head. "I ain't sure." She slid her gaze to Hannah, then back to her son. "I'm gonna do everything I can, but it'll be up to the judge when."

Andy puffed out his chest. "I'll tell him I want to come home. He'll listen to me."

"Baby, I'm sure he will, but I hafta do a couple of things before we go in front of the judge. Then ya can tell him what ya want. Okay?"

Andy frowned. "I guess so."

"Good. I know I can count on ya, baby." Lisa drew her son to her and held him tightly.

Emotions clogged Hannah's throat. She swallowed several times before she said, "Andy, I'm sure we'll be able to arrange for your mother to come see you at the refuge. You can show her your room. She can meet your friends."

Hope flared in the boy's expression. "Yes. How about tomorrow?"

Hannah rose. "Let me see what I can arrange, Andy. It may have to be some time next week."

The light in his eyes dimmed. "Promise?"

"I can promise you I'll do everything I can to make it happen." *Please, Lord, help me to keep that promise.*

Jacob leaned into the railing on the porch of the cottage and stared up at the crystal clear night sky, littered with hundreds of stars. The cool fall air soothed his frustration some as he waited to speak with Hannah after the children were in bed. He didn't want to have this conversation where the kids might overhear.

Not only didn't Lisa Morgan get hauled down to the police station for defying a court order, but now Hannah was making arrangements for the woman to see Andy here at the refuge. Dinner, no less, in two nights! And worse, she'd persuaded Laura and Peter to go along with this crazy plan of hers.

The sound of the front door opening and closing drew Jacob up straight, but he didn't look at Hannah. He kept his gaze glued on the stars.

Lord, give me the right words to convince Hannah of the folly of getting Andy and his mother together except in a courtroom.

"You wanted to talk to me." Hannah moved to the other side of the steps and leaned against the post. "I'm tired so can we make this quick."

He clenched the wooden railing. Patience. He faced her, a couple of yards between them, her expression hidden in the shadows of evening, although Jacob didn't need to see her to imagine her glower. "We need to talk about Andy and his mother."

"No, we don't. You may be on the board, but I was hired to be the manager." She pushed away from the post, her posture stiff. "That means I run the refuge. I have Peter and Laura's support."

Which he intended to change the first opportunity he got a chance to speak with them. "And what happens when Lisa Morgan takes Andy again and harms him. Or comes to the cottage on drugs. Or lets her son down by not showing up when she's supposed to."

"She isn't the one who hurt Andy. It was her boyfriend who isn't around anymore."

"She allowed it to happen. That's the same thing in my book."

"One of the calls I placed this afternoon was to a drug-rehab facility. I got her in. She can start the program next week."

Jacob snorted. "So she goes through the motions of getting clean, and the second she gets Andy back she's taking drugs again and hooking up with that boyfriend or some other who is equally abusive to Andy." As much as he tried to keep visions of his past from flashing across his mind, he couldn't. The first time his mother had come out of drug rehab, he'd had such hope that she would stay clean. She'd lasted one whole day. He could still remember as if it were yesterday finding her passed out on the floor in the living room. "Then where does that leave Andy?"

"I have to try."

"Why?"

"Andy loves his mother. He wants to be with her. He told me he called her to come to the zoo." She could never share the pain she had gone through when her family had fallen apart. Even though it was under different circumstances and she had continued to live with her mom, she'd essentially lost her that day her older brother was killed. And the person responsible stood in front of her. She tamped down on the words of anger she suddenly wanted to shout at him. They would do no good. She needed to learn to work with this man—somehow.

"He'll get over it."

Hannah drew in a sharp breath. "How can you say something like that?"

"Because I did."

His whispered words hung in the air between them. Did she hear him right? She stepped closer. "What did you say?"

He pivoted away from her, gripping the railing. "My mother was like Lisa Morgan. On drugs. Nothing else was important to her. Certainly not me. Or where the rent and food money was going to come from. And when she didn't have enough money for her drugs, she took her frustration out on me with a fist or a belt."

Her anger disintegrated at the anguish in his voice. She wasn't even sure he was aware of it lacing each word. A strong impulse to comfort inundated her. She held her ground for a few seconds before she covered the distance between them to stand next to Jacob.

"I'm sorry," she whispered, meaning it. She caught a glimpse of his expression in the moonlight. Painful memories etched deep lines into his face as though he was reliving his past.

Finally as if he realized he had an audience to witness his agony, he blinked and shook his head. "I don't need your pity. All I want from you is to put a stop to getting Andy together with his mother."

As though she had no control over her actions, she lay her hand on his arm. "I can't. Andy is so excited about his mother coming to dinner."

He jerked away. "What you mean is, you won't! You want to try some little social experiment to see if it works." He thrust his face close to hers. "You're experimenting with a young boy's life."

Hannah stepped back. "And you're not? What happened to you was a tragedy, but that doesn't mean it will happen to everyone in the same situation. What if Lisa can successfully kick the habit? Wouldn't Andy be better off with his mother rather than in the foster-care system, possibly never adopted? We owe it to him to try."

"We owe him protection and a quality life."

"I'm not going into this with my eyes closed. I know what can happen and I plan to be there every step of the way."

"And I plan on being here, too. Plan to have another person at dinner on Sunday night."

"Fine. You're welcome to come here anytime." The second she said it she wanted to take it back. That meant she would see him more than an occasional call to the doctor's office or a social visit from him to see the children every once and a while.

"Good, because I'll be here a lot."

Her earlier exhaustion assailed her. Her legs weak, she sank down onto the steps. Her emotions had taken a beating today, and it looked as if it wouldn't be over with for a long time. Again she thought about walking away from the job, but then she remembered Andy's huge smile at bedtime because his mother was coming to visit him in a few days. He'd already started cleaning his room so it would be perfect for her.

"You know, I'm not going into this lightly. I told you about my involvement in a program where the children lived in the same neighborhood as their parents and saw them frequently in supervised situations. The program also worked with the parents, helping them address whatever forced the state to take their children, whether it was anger management, drug or alcohol abuse."

He sat next to her. "And what was the success rate?"

"Thirty to forty percent."

"What happened to the sixty or seventy percent it didn't work with?"

"Other arrangements were made for them. No one was left in a bad situation."

"That you know of."

"The program had long-term follow-up built into it. When I interviewed with Laura and Peter, they knew my desire to try something like that here."

His expression displayed surprise. "They did?"

"We need to explore all opportunities for the children. One is trying to get them back with their parents. Do you feel every child in the foster-care system should never go back home?"

"No."

"Then why are you against this?"

He closed his eyes for a few seconds. "Because Andy could be me."

"But he isn't."

"That remains to be seen." Jacob shot to his feet and dug into his pocket for his keys. "I'll be here Sunday." He stalked toward his old car in front of the cottage.

She sat on the porch step watching him drive away, stunned by what she had discovered about the person she had grown up hating. He had been abused. It didn't change what he had done to her brother, but it did alter her feelings. It was hard to look at him and not see what he must have gone through as a child.

She thought about a sermon she'd heard a few months ago about being careful not to judge another. How could we know what that person had gone through unless we walked in his shoes? Until this moment she hadn't really contemplated its true meaning.

Chapter Five

"You're early for dinner." Hannah glanced up from reading the paperwork needed for Lisa's rehab facility.

Jacob fit his long length into the small chair to the side of her desk. "I promised some of the kids I'd play touch football. The day has turned out to be great so here I am." He spread his arms wide.

Indeed, he was, looking ruggedly handsome with tousled hair and warm brown eyes. "Who?"

"Some of the older boys in the other cottage, but Gabe and Terry want to play, too."

"Is that safe?" She stacked the papers to the side to give to Lisa later.

He grinned, his two dimples appearing. "I'll protect them. They've always watched before, but both boys love football so I said yes."

"Still…aren't they a little young to play?"

He pushed to his feet, giving her a wink. "I

promise they will be fine, and you know I don't break a promise."

"You can't control everything."

The merriment in his eyes died. "I, more than most, realize that. Your life can change instantly and take you in a completely opposite direction than you ever imagined." He headed for the door. "I'm going to have a few words with the older guys about making sure Gabe and Terry have fun but aren't hurt." He peered back at her. "Okay?"

"Yes," she said as he disappeared out into the hall.

She had a report to read, but maybe she should go watch the game just in case something unforeseen happened. *Yeah, right. Is that the only reason?*

She had to admit to herself that since Friday night, when Jacob had told her something about his childhood, she hadn't been able to get the man out of her mind. And only a moment before he'd referred to life changing so quickly. Perhaps he hadn't walked away from the wreck unscathed.

She left her office and went in search of the touch-football game. She found a group of kids in the area between the two cottages and among them was Jacob giving instructions on the rules. Gabe and Terry, smaller than the other boys, flanked Jacob. How good he was with the children was reconfirmed as she watched.

"Will Terry and Gabe be all right?" Susie asked, coming to Hannah's side with Nancy.

"Dr. Jacob told me they would be."

"Then they will. Good. I wouldn't want anything to happen to them. Terry wants to try out for the basketball team at school and tryouts are next week."

"He didn't say anything to me. When?" She shouldn't be surprised Susie knew before her. The young girl was a mother hen to the kids in the cottage.

Susie shrugged. "He probably forgot. It isn't until Thursday after school.

Nancy tugged on Hannah's hand. "I'm gonna be a cheerleader. Susie taught me some cheers."

Hannah scanned the children assembled. "Where's Andy? I thought he would be out here in the thick of things, even if he can't play."

"He's cleaning his room—again." Susie clapped as the two teams lined up, with Nancy mimicking the older girl's action.

"I'll go check on him and get him to come out here." Hannah hurried toward the house. She didn't want to miss the game—in case there was a problem. *Yeah, sure. You're fooling yourself again. Jacob Hartman is the reason you're out here and not inside reading that report you need to go through.*

In the cottage she discovered Andy folding his clothes in his drawer and having a hard time with only one hand. "Hey, there's a big game being played outside. Dr. Jacob is here and in the middle of it."

"I know. But my room isn't clean enough." Andy attempted to refold the T-shirt.

Hannah surveyed the spotless area. She walked

to Andy and took the piece of clothing. "You want to talk?"

"Nope. I've got to get this done." He averted his gaze.

"This looks great."

"It isn't good enough yet."

She thought about leaving him alone, but the quaver in his voice demanded her full attention. She drew him around to face her. "Andy, I won't lie to you. You can't do anything else to this room to make it better. I wish all the children's bedrooms were this clean."

"But—but it's got to be perfect for Mom."

"Why, hon?"

"Mom needs to know I can keep our place clean."

Hannah tugged Andy to the bed and sat with him next to her. "Then she will know. Why do you feel that way?"

"'Cause—" he sniffled "—'cause her boyfriend got mad at me for leaving the cereal out. He started to hit me when she came in between us. He hurt her instead."

She settled her arm along his shoulders. "He moved out so you won't have to worry about him."

Sniffing, Andy wiped his sleeve across his face. "But he could come back. He's left before and come back."

Hannah hugged the boy to her. "Let's not worry about that right now. I want you to have a good time showing your mother around and introducing her to your friends." She stood. "C'mon, let's see what everyone else is doing."

Andy remained seated. "Can I tell ya a secret?"

"Sure."

"He gave Mom money to live on. She's tried some jobs, but they never last long. Do you think if I get a job it'll help? 'Course, I can't quit school. Mom didn't finish, and she told me how important it is I do."

Staring down at Andy, Hannah felt she was talking to a little adult. Her heart broke at the worry and seriousness she saw in the boy's eyes. "Tell you what. If you promise me you won't worry about finding a job, I'll help your mother find one after she gets out of drug rehab. Okay?"

"You will?" Joy flooded his face as he leaped to his feet. "That would be so good!"

She held out her hand. "Let's go see what's going on outside."

As they strolled toward the yard between the cottages, Hannah mulled over what Andy had told her. She knew Lisa wasn't well educated from the way she talked. Getting her help with her drug problem was only the beginning of what Lisa and Andy would need if reuniting the family were going to work. She hadn't really thought beyond getting Lisa through a drug-rehab program. Maybe she was naive. Jacob certainly thought so.

I'm just going to have to prove him wrong.

Outside Hannah positioned herself on the sidelines of the makeshift football field with Andy on one side and Nancy on the other. Watching Jacob playing with the children, Hannah decided he was a big kid at heart. The laughter and ribbing filled the cool fall air. Before she knew it the sun began to slip down the sky toward the western horizon.

"Shouldn't Mom be here by now?" Andy asked as the losing team shook hands with the winners.

Hannah checked her watch. "She's only a few minutes late." *Please, Lord, let Lisa show up. If she doesn't…* Hannah didn't have any words to express her regret if the woman didn't come.

Jacob jogged toward her, his shirttail hanging out of his jeans, some dirt smudges on his face, his hair tousled even more than usual where some of the children tackled him to the ground at the end. Gabe and Terry had hung back until all the bigger kids were on the pile then they joined the others on top.

Jacob peered toward the road that led to the cottages and mouthed the words, "Not here?" so that Andy, who was staring at the same road, wouldn't hear.

She shook her head. "Everyone needs to clean up. Dinner is in an hour." She eyed Jacob and his smudges. "Including you."

"I brought an extra shirt in case something like this happened, which it does every time." With a wink, he loped toward his car.

"What if something happened to Mom?"

Hannah put her hands on Andy's shoulders and pulled his attention away from the road by blocking his view. "We have an hour until we eat. Don't you know women are notorious for being late to important events. We have to make our grand entrance."

"Ya think that's it?"

I hope so. "Yes," she said, and sent up another prayer.

She and the children walked toward the cottage as Jacob joined them, carrying his clean shirt. He slipped into the house ahead of them and made his way to the bathroom off the kitchen. The kids dispersed to their bedrooms to clean up. Hannah stood in the foyer with Andy, Nancy and Susie.

The boy glanced back at the front door. "I'm gonna wait out on the porch."

After Andy left, Hannah said to Susie, "Will you make sure everyone really cleans up? I'll be outside with Andy."

"Sure. I hope his mother comes. He's been so excited." Susie took Nancy's hand to lead her back to the bedrooms.

Nancy stuck her thumb into her mouth and began to suck it. Hannah watched them disappear down the hall, wondering why the five-year-old was sucking her thumb. She hadn't seen that before, and it now worried Hannah.

Out on the porch Hannah eased down next to Andy on the front steps. He cradled his chin in his palm and stared at the road. Her heart contracted at the forlorn look on the boy's face. *Maybe Jacob is right. I should have left well enough alone.*

She searched her mind for something to make the situation better when she heard the door open and close. She glanced back at Jacob, who came to sit on the other side of Andy. She saw no reproach in Jacob's expression, which surprised her. Lisa was a half an hour late, and a lot of people would now be gloating about how she had been wrong.

"You know, I want a rematch tonight. I can't let Gabe's win stand. Want to join us in the game, Andy?" Jacob lounged back, propping himself up with his elbows and appearing as though he had not care in the world.

Until you looked into his eyes, Hannah thought, *and glimpsed the worry deep in their depths.*

"Can Mom play, too?"

It took Jacob several heartbeats to answer, "Sure." But again nothing was betrayed in his expression or tone of voice.

Andy jumped to his feet. "Look! She's coming." He pointed toward a woman walking down the road toward the cottage.

Before Hannah could say anything, the boy leaped off the steps and raced toward his mother. Relief trembled through Hannah at the sight of the woman. Lisa scooped up Andy into a bear hug, then looped her arm around him.

"She came," Hannah murmured, tears smarting her eyes.

The silence from Jacob electrified the air. She resisted the urge to look at him and instead relished this step forward in Andy and his mother's relationship. *Maybe my plan will work after all. Thank you, Lord.*

"I'm glad she's here," Jacob finally said, straightening.

When Hannah peered at him, relief replaced the worry in his gaze as he observed the pair make their way toward him. She realized in that moment that he wanted what was best for Andy, even if he was wrong. They didn't agree what was best, but they had a common goal: Andy's safety and happiness. There was a part of her that was unnerved that she would have another thing in common with Jacob, but she couldn't deny it. In that moment she felt close to him, and that sensation surprised her even more than his earlier lack of reproach.

Hannah brushed her hand across her cheek and rose as mother and child approached. "It's so good to see you, Lisa, but how did you get here?"

Lisa stopped at the bottom of the steps with Andy cradled against her side. "I walked from the bus stop."

"That's two miles away." She couldn't believe she hadn't thought about the fact that Lisa might not have transportation out to the farm.

Andy's mother grinned. "I need to get in shape. It took me a bit longer than I thought." She splayed her hand across her chest. "I had to rest about halfway. But I'm here now."

Hannah stepped to the side. "Welcome to Stone's Refuge. The children are waiting inside to meet you."

Andy took his mother's hand and led her into the house. Jacob nodded his head and indicated Hannah go through the entrance before him. She did and felt his gaze burning a hole into her back. She paused in the foyer to watch the children greet Andy's mother in the living room. The only one who didn't was Nancy. She hung back with her thumb in her mouth and her gaze trained on the floor by her feet.

"What's wrong with Nancy?" Jacob whispered into her ear.

Nearly jumping, Hannah gasped and spun around. She'd been so focused on Andy and his mother that Hannah hadn't heard Jacob approach from behind her. "Give a gal some warning."

"Sorry. I haven't seen Nancy sucking her thumb before. When did it start?"

"I think this afternoon. At least that's the first time I've seen it since I've been here."

Jacob frowned and peered at the little girl, still off to the side while everyone else was crowded around Andy and Lisa, all trying to talk at the same time. A dazed look appeared in Lisa's eyes.

Hannah moved forward. "Andy, why don't you give your mother a tour of the house and show her your bedroom? Dinner will be in half an hour."

En masse the group started for the back of the house. Except for Nancy. She stayed in the living room, continuing to stare at the floor. Hannah covered the distance between her and the little girl and knelt in front of Nancy.

"What's wrong?"

With thumb still in her mouth, Nancy shook her head.

"Are you sure I can't help you with something?"

She nodded, hugging her arms to her, her eyes still downcast.

"Well, I sure could use someone to help me set the table. Will you, Nancy?"

"Yes," the child mumbled around her thumb.

"I'll help, too." Jacob came up to join them.

"Great. We'll get it done in no time." Hannah held out her hand for Nancy to take. She did.

Jacob flanked the little girl on the other side and extended his palm to her. She stared at it for a long second before removing her thumb from her mouth and grasping him. "Are you looking forward to going back to kindergarten tomorrow after your fall break?"

"My teacher's so nice. I'm gonna tell her about the zoo and the pla—mingos."

Hannah left Nancy and Jacob in the dining room while she went into the kitchen to get the place mats and dishes. Arms loaded, she backed through the swinging door and nearly collided with Jacob. Nancy giggled. He took the plates, set them on the table, then passed the mats to the girl.

"I'll do these while you put those down." Jacob gestured toward the mats held in Nancy's hands.

Hannah hurried back for the rest of the dishes. In ten minutes the dining-room table was set. She stood back with Jacob on one side and Nancy on the other. "We're a good team. Next time I need some help, I'll have to ask you, Nancy."

She peered up at Hannah, a question in her eyes. "How about Dr. Jacob? He helped."

"Yeah, a team has to stick together," Jacob said with a laugh.

"Him, too." The heat rose in Hannah's cheeks. The idea of them being a team wasn't as disturbing as she would have once thought.

Hannah examined the piece of paper Nancy held up. "I like your flamingo. Are you going to share it with your class tomorrow?"

The little girl nodded. "Just in case they don't know what one looks like."

"Well, they will now with this picture." Hannah tilted her head, tapping her chin with her finger. "You know, it seems I remember someone has a birthday coming up."

"Me!" Nancy pointed to herself. "I'll be six in four days."

"We'll have to think of something special to celebrate such an important birthday."

Shouts of victory permeated the living room. Hannah glanced toward the game table by the bay window.

Andy stood by his chair, pumping his good arm into the air and dancing around in a circle. "I won finally!"

"Why don't you take this back to your room and start getting ready for bed." Hannah handed the paper to Nancy.

"But I'm not tired."

"Tomorrow will be here soon enough."

As Nancy trudged from the room, Hannah rose and walked to the table where Jacob sat with Andy, Gabe and Lisa playing a board game. Gabe began to set up the pieces again for another game.

"Sorry, guys. It's time for bed."

Moans greeted Hannah's announcement.

"But Dr. Jacob hasn't won yet," Gabe said, continuing to put the pieces on the board.

"Too bad. He'll have to win some other day."

Gabe pouted. "But—"

"Gabe, Hannah is right. This just means we'll have to play again at a later date." Jacob picked up the game box.

Andy jumped to his feet. "Mom, can you put me to bed?"

Lisa peered at Hannah. "If it's okay?"

"That's great. I'll help Jacob clean up while you two boys get into your pajamas." Hannah surveyed the other children in the room. "That goes for everyone." As the kids filed into the hallway, Hannah stopped Lisa. "May I have a word with you?"

"Andy, I'll be there in a sec." Lisa waved her son on.

"How are you getting home?" Hannah asked when the room emptied of children.

"Walking to the bus stop. The last one is at ten."

"I'll drive you home. I don't want you walking at night on the highway."

"I don't want ya to go—"

"I'll take you home. I have to go that way." Jacob boxed up the last piece of the game and put it in the cabinet.

Appreciation shone in Lisa's expression. "I won't be long. I'll go say good-night to Andy."

"I'll go with you." Jacob started after Andy's mother.

Hannah halted him. She waited until Lisa had disappeared from the room before asking, "Are you sure? I don't mind taking her. Meg is still here to watch the children. I won't be gone long."

"No, I need to get to know her better. This will be a good opportunity to see what her intentions are toward Andy."

"Maybe I'd better take her after all."

He chuckled. "Afraid I'll scare her away?"

"No."

"Good, because if I can then she shouldn't be involved with Andy and finding out now would be better than later."

Hannah's eyes widened. "You're going to interrogate her?"

He saw the concern in her gaze that quickly evolved into a frown. "No, I'll be on my best behavior. I offered because there really is no reason for you to drive her into town." Shrugging, he flashed her a grin. "I'm going that way."

"Just so you'll know, tomorrow I'm taking her to the rehab facility to begin the program. Don't frighten her away."

"Who, me?" He thumped his chest. "I'm wounded. I want it to work out for Andy. I just don't think it will." He held up a hand to ward off her protest. "But I'm willing to go along so long as Andy isn't hurt. The second he is—"

Hannah walked toward the entrance, cutting off his words with a wave. "I have the child's best interest at heart, so you don't have to threaten me."

"Excuse me?"

She wheeled around at the door. "What are you going to do? Come riding in on your white steed and save the day?"

"Why, Ms. Smith, I do believe that's sarcasm I hear in your voice."

She put her hand on her waist. "I think we can agree on disagreeing about how to handle Lisa and Andy."

"Hey, I'm willing to give it a try. I behaved at dinner."

Her other hand went to her waist. "If you call behaving, giving the poor woman the third degree, then, yes, you behaved like a perfect gentleman."

"Ouch! I do believe your barb found its mark." He flattened his palm over his heart. "I wanted to know how she was going to support Andy."

"I could have told you she doesn't have a job. I intend to find her one."

"You do?"

"Well, yes, when she's completed the drug-rehab program. Do you know of anyone who might hire her?"

"Not off the top of my head. But let's wait and see what happens in a few weeks before you go out pounding the pavement looking for a job for Andy's mom." He strode to her, gave her a wink and headed down the hallway. "You may not have to worry about it."

Jacob heard Hannah's gasp and chuckled. He enjoyed ruffling her feathers, so to speak. He expected Hannah to follow him to Andy's room, but when he stopped at the boy's door, she still hadn't come down the corridor. Disappointment fluttered through him.

Cradled against his mother, Andy sat on his bed in his pajamas, listening to her read a story. When she closed the book, Andy said, "Again."

Lisa glanced toward Jacob. "I have to go, but I'll be back."

"Promise."

"If it was just me, I would, but the judge makes the decisions now. I hope so." Emotions thickened her voice.

"I love you, Mommy." Andy threw his arms around her.

She kissed the top of his head, then stood. "I'm gonna get help, Andy. This time it'll work."

This time? As Jacob had thought, Lisa had gone through rehab before and it hadn't been successful. He backed away, not wanting Andy to see anything in his expression. But in his mind Lisa represented his mother and his concern skyrocketed.

Jacob waited in the front foyer for the woman to emerge from the back. She said goodbye to Hannah then approached him. He wrenched open the door and stepped to the side to allow Andy's mother to go first. When he glanced toward Hannah, her look communicated a plea for understanding, as though she could read the war going on inside of him.

After asking for Lisa's address, Jacob fell silent on the drive into town. Memories of his own mother assailed him. He'd known he would be reminded of his childhood when he chose to work with children in the foster-care system. He'd thought he was prepared and usually he was. But not this time. His grip on the steering wheel tightened.

Jacob pulled to the curb in an area of town that had seen better days. Trash littered the streets and even with the windows rolled up, a decaying smell seeped into the car. "You live around here?"

Lisa grasped the door handle. "No, but I can catch a bus on the corner."

He scanned the area and wondered who or what lurked in the darkness between the buildings. "I said I'd drive you home, and I meant all the way."

"But—"

His gaze fixed on a broken-out storefront window. A movement inside the abandoned building made him press his foot on the accelerator. "I can't leave you here. It's too dangerous. Where are you staying?"

Silence.

Jacob slid a glance toward Lisa who stared at her hands in her lap. "You were staying back there?"

She nodded.

"Where?"

"In one of the buildings."

"You're homeless."

"It was my boyfriend's place Andy and I was staying at. He came back last night and kicked me out."

"So now you don't have anywhere to live?"

"No."

When Jacob turned onto a well-lit street, he sighed with relief. "How did you get to the zoo?"

"By bus."

Jacob made another turn, heading into the heart of the city. "I'm taking you to a shelter that's run by a couple from my church. They're good people. You'll be safe there." Again he looked toward Lisa and caught the tears streaking down her cheeks. "Okay?"

"Yeah," she mumbled, and dropped her head.

Something deep in his heart cracked open when he glimpsed Lisa's hurt. "I'll let Hannah know where you're staying so she can come there to pick you up tomorrow."

Her sobs sounded in the quiet, and another fissure opened up in his heart. Conflicting emotions concerning Lisa and her situation swirled through him.

"Why are ya being so nice? Ya don't like me," Lisa finally said between sniffles.

"For Andy." Jacob pulled into a parking space at the side of the shelter in downtown Cimarron City near his church.

Lisa lifted her head. "I love my son."

"Enough to stop taking drugs?"

She blinked, loosening several more tears. "Yeah."

"I'll be praying you do." Jacob opened his door, realizing as he slid out of the car that he meant every word. He would pray for Lisa's recovery. In the past he'd always thought of the child, never the parent in the situation. He was finding out there were two sides to a story.

Inside the shelter connected to his church, Jacob greeted Herb and Vickie Braun. "Lisa needs a place to stay for the night."

"We've got a bed. I'll show you the way." Vickie gestured toward a hallway that led to the sleeping area.

As the two women left the large hall where the residents ate their meals, Herb slapped Jacob on the back. "I wondered when we'd see you again. We've missed you down here."

"I've been so busy with Stone's Refuge and my practice."

"Eighteen children can keep you hopping. What you, Peter and Noah have done is great and definitely needed."

"We've appreciated you keeping an eye out for any children in need of a safe place to stay." Jacob walked toward the front door. "In a few months the third house will be finished."

"We'll take care of Lisa. She'll have a place to stay for as long as she needs it."

Back in his car Jacob rested his forehead on the steering wheel. He hadn't wanted to tell Herb the reason he didn't volunteer at the shelter, as many did from the church, was that it hit too close to home. There had been many times he had stayed in a shelter with his mother, but none were as safe and nice as this one. He'd comforted himself with financially supporting the place, but he knew now he should do something more. He needed to face his past and deal with it. He'd been running for a long time.

He started his car and drove toward his apartment near his practice. Emotionally exhausted, he plodded into the building and punched the elevator for his floor. Five minutes later, he plunked down on his bed and lay back, still fully dressed. He needed to get up and check his messages, then finish making some notes on a case, but a bone-weary tiredness held him pinned to the mattress. His eyes slid closed….

Darkness loomed before Jacob, rushing toward him.

"Let's go faster," Kevin said, turning the radio up louder, the music pulsating in the air.

"I can't see well." Jacob squinted his eyes as if that would improve his vision so he could see out the windshield better.

His friend shifted toward him until he spied the dashboard. "You're only going forty. What's the point taking Dad's car if we don't do something fun?"

"You're the one who wanted to come out here." Jacob's gaze swept the road in front of him, then the sides he could barely make out. Piles of snow still lined the highway.

"Yeah, so we could put the pedal to the metal. If you don't want to, I'll drive again."

To keep his friend quiet, Jacob increased the speed to forty-five but looked for a place to pull over so Kevin could drive. Suddenly he lost control of the car, the darkness spiraling around him. Screams pierced the quiet, sounds of glass breaking….

Jacob shot up in bed, sweat drenching him. His whole body shook from the nightmare that had plagued him for years—one of his punishments for surviving the wreck that killed Kevin.

Chapter Six

Hannah stared at the shelves full of medical books with titles that made her head spin. Why was she standing in the middle of Jacob's office waiting for him? She rotated around to grab her purse on the chair and leave before he came into the room. As she gripped the leather handle, the door opened, and she knew she was stuck.

"I was surprised to hear you were here." Jacob's smile wiped the weariness from his face. "I'm assuming everything is all right at the refuge or Teresa would have said something about it to me."

"Everything's fine. I just dropped Lisa off at the rehab center and wanted to stop by and thank you for finding a place for her to stay last night." Hannah released her strap and straightened. "I didn't realize she was living on the street. She didn't say anything to me about that."

"It was nothing. At this time of year Herb and

Vickie always have a spare bed at the shelter. Now, if it had been winter, it might have been different."

"I should have figured something like that had happened to her when she mentioned she wasn't working. I'm learning." She attempted a smile that quivered. "At least she has a place to stay for the next few weeks."

"If she stays there." Jacob dropped a file on his desk, releasing a long sigh.

Exhaustion, etching tiny lines into his face, sparked her compassion. "Long day?"

"Nonstop since I arrived this morning. The beginning of the flu season."

"Don't mention that word to me. I have eighteen children to keep healthy. I know you gave them a flu shot, but that's not the only illness they can get."

"As I well know. You've got your work cut out for you." He leaned back against his desk and folded his arms over his chest.

"I think you're right."

His eyebrows shot up. "You're admitting I might be right. Hold it right there while I get my recorder and you can repeat it for the microphone."

"Funny. I could say the same thing about you. You think I'm naive and idealistic."

"You are, but the world needs all kinds of people."

"So they don't all have to be cynical and realistic?"

He thrust away from the desk. "I hope not or we are in big trouble. Are you hungry?"

"Why?"

"Now, that question sounds cynical." He grinned. "Because I am hungry, and I'd like to take you to Noah's restaurant for dinner."

"According to all the kids that's their favorite place to eat."

"According to Noah it's the best in the whole Southwest."

"Will your friend be there?"

"If he's not out on a date, he's usually there. He's worse than me about working all the time. The one on Columbia Street was his first restaurant so he has a soft spot for it." Jacob snatched his jacket from the peg on the back of the door and slipped it on.

"I know he's a board member of the Henderson Foundation, but I haven't met him yet." Hannah exited the office first, into the dim light of the hallway.

Jacob came up behind her. "I guess everyone skedaddled out of here the first chance they got. Did I tell you it has been a long, crazy day?"

"I believe you mentioned that fact." She was very aware they were probably the only two people left in his suite of offices.

His chuckle peppered the air, making Hannah even more conscious of the fact they were alone. She'd come by to thank him for helping Lisa, and now she was going to dinner with him. How had that happened? For a moment in his office she'd forgotten who Jacob was. She needed to remember it at all times.

Hannah hurried her step toward the outer door.

When she emerged from the building, she headed for her vehicle. "I'll follow you. I'm not sure where the restaurant is."

"Fine." Jacob unlocked his car door and climbed inside.

While she dug her keys out of her pocket, Hannah listened to him try to start his engine. A cranking sound that grated down her spine cut into the silence, then nothing. Dead. She peered over her shoulder as he tried again. Frustration marked his expression as he exited his vehicle.

He strode to her. "I knew it was only a matter of time before she died. I was hoping to get a few more months out of her."

"Maybe you can get it fixed."

"That baby was my first car, and I need to say goodbye to her. Can I hitch a ride with you?"

"Sure." Why hadn't she brought the van? She stared at her very small car that practically forced people to sit on top of each other. "Do you still want to go to dinner?"

"A guy's got to eat, and if you could see my refrigerator, you'd take pity on me. I don't live too far from the restaurant or here. In fact, it'll be on your way to the refuge. If you need to get back, we can skip dinner and grab a quick bite at some fast-food joint."

A way out. She pushed the button to unlock her doors. "I don't have to be back at the refuge for a while. Laura relieves me on Monday to give me some time off."

"That's great." He walked around the back of her

vehicle and slipped into the passenger seat. "After rushing around all day, it would be nice to kick back and have a relaxing dinner."

Oh, good. She blew her one chance to end the evening early. She didn't understand what was going on with her. A week ago she would have avoided any time spent in Jacob's company. But that was before she had gotten to know him better. Nothing was ever black-and-white and the gray areas were tripping her up.

Her car purred to life, and she pulled out of the parking lot onto the still-busy street. In the small confines she smelled his distinctive male scent, laced with a hint of the forest. Too cozy for her peace of mind.

"Turn right at the next corner and go three blocks. The restaurant is on the left side of the road."

His deep, baritone voice, edged with exhaustion, shivered through her. "Do you eat at your friend's a lot?"

"Probably once a week. Sometimes I bring the kids from the refuge."

"You do?" She was constantly discovering he was more involved in the children's lives than she had ever thought possible. "All of them?"

"Not usually. I rotate six different ones each time. I don't want to play favorites and cause any problems."

"Do you have a favorite?"

"I try not to. They all need love and understanding. But…"

His voice faded into the quiet.

"What? Fess up. Which one has stolen your heart?"

"It's hard for me not to be drawn to Andy."

Although she thought she knew the answer, she asked, "Why?" She pulled into a parking space next to the restaurant and looked at him, the light from the building washing over his face.

"Because he reminds me of myself when I was his age."

"And that's why you're being so hard on Lisa." Knowing how he felt about Andy's mother, she should be surprised he had taken the time to help her the evening before, but she wasn't, because the more she got acquainted with Jacob the more she realized that would be exactly what he would do.

"No, I'm skeptical of her motives because I've seen that kind of situation before and it didn't turn out well."

"I'm sorry about your mother, but Lisa isn't her."

"It's not just my mother I'm talking about. I've seen a lot over the years as a foster child and a doctor."

"Were there any situations where a parent was able to stay off drugs and take care of her child?"

He thought for a moment and answered, "One of my friends was lucky."

She placed her hand on the handle. "Then maybe Andy and Lisa will be like that one." She opened the door and left her car before they got into a heated discussion as they had in the past when they'd talked about the little boy's situation.

Inside the restaurant wonderful smells of spices, tomato and meats caused Hannah's mouth to water. "I didn't realize how hungry I was until now."

After they ordered at the counter, Jacob found them a table in the back in a less-crowded section and pulled out her chair as if they were on a date. She stared at it for a few seconds before she sat and let him scoot it forward. His hand brushed her shoulder as he came around to his side, and she nearly jumped at the casual touch.

Get a grip. This is not a date. It is simply two people who are acquainted sharing a meal. It could never be anything more than that.

"They're usually pretty fast here, so it shouldn't be long before they bring us our pizzas. And this is my treat."

"You don't have to," she immediately said, not liking how that made this sound more like a date.

"Yes, I do. You're helping me out, and I always pay my debts."

"Is that why you have a car that should have seen the inside of a salvage yard a long time ago?"

For a couple of heartbeats his jaw tightened, a veil falling over his expression. Then it was gone and he grinned. "Contrary to how a lot of men feel about their cars, I don't care what I drive. I wanted to pay off my educational loans before I took on any more debt."

"When will you be finished?"

"In a few months." He looked beyond her and his smile grew. "I wondered if you were here. Hannah, this is Noah, the guy who is responsible for adding at least five pounds to my waist."

A tall man with long brown hair pulled back with a leather strap paused at the table. "I must admit this isn't something I see often. I had to come out and meet the woman who could make my friend stop long enough to go out on a date."

Hannah shook Noah's hand. "Oh, this isn't a date. We're just…" How did she describe what they were?

"We're friends enjoying some pizza," Jacob finished for her.

"Sure. Sorry about the mistake." Noah's gaze danced with merriment as it lit upon first Jacob then Hannah.

"Hannah is the new manager at Stone's Refuge. Why she was interested in meeting you, I don't know."

Noah laughed. "She probably heard of my charming personality."

"No doubt," Jacob grumbled good-naturedly. "Are you leaving?"

Noah's laughter increased. "I can take a hint. You don't have to wound me."

"I couldn't wound you. Your hide is too thick."

The restaurant owner shifted his attention to Hannah. "Don't listen to a thing he says. He doesn't know how to have fun. He's too busy working all the time." He took her hand. "It was nice meeting you. I'm sure I'll see you around the farm."

As Noah strolled away, Hannah turned to Jacob. "Did you tell me y'all are friends?"

"Afraid so. Actually Noah and Peter are like brothers to me."

"Then that accounts for your ribbing."

"You sound like someone who has siblings. A brother or sister?"

The reminder of Kevin struck her low. She struggled to keep herself composed while she sat across from the man who caused her brother's death. Trembling, she clutched the sides of the chair.

"Excuse me." She bolted to her feet and searched for the restrooms.

Seeing the sign across the room, she quickly fled the table. Inside she locked the door and collapsed back against it. When she lifted her gaze to the mirror over the sink, she saw two large eyes, full of sorrow, staring back at her. She covered her cheeks, the heat beneath her fingertips searing them. His question had taken her by surprise and dumped her past in her lap.

She crossed to the sink and splashed cold water on her face, then examined her reflection in the mirror for any telltale signs of her grief. Blue eyes filled her vision, pain lurking just beneath the surface. She stamped it down.

She needed to get through dinner. Thinking about Kevin—the fact she had never been able to say goodbye to him because her parents wouldn't let her go to the funeral—was something she couldn't afford to do right now.

"You can do this." She blew out a breath of air, lifting her bangs from her forehead, and left the restroom.

Jacob stood when she approached. Worry knitted his forehead. "Are you all right?"

She took her chair, noticing that the pizzas had been delivered while she was gone. "I'm fine."

"Did I say something wrong?"

"I did have an older brother. He's dead. Your question took me by surprise. That's all."

He covered her hand on the table. "I'm so sorry about your brother."

Somehow she managed not to jerk back. She forced a smile to her lips and said, "I'm hungry. Let's dig in."

As Hannah took her first bite of the Canadian bacon slice, she knew what she had to do soon. She needed to go out to her brother's grave site. She needed to say goodbye.

The next afternoon at the cemetery, Hannah's steps slowed as she neared where her brother lay at rest. A vase of brightly colored flowers drew her immediate attention. Where had those come from? She had no relatives living in Cimarron City.

Hannah put her mum plant next to the vase, then moved back. The bright sunlight bathed her in warmth she desperately needed. Hugging her arms to her, she wished she had worn a heavier sweater. The north wind cut through her, and she positioned herself behind the large oak that shaded the area, its trunk blocking the worst of the chill.

"Kevin, I'm sorry I told on you that last day. If you hadn't gotten in trouble with Dad, you might not have gone out joyriding that night. If I had only known…" The lump in her throat prevented her from saying the rest aloud. But for years she had wondered: if she hadn't tattled on her brother, would that have changed the outcome of that night? That was something she would never know the answer to.

Lord, I need Your help in forgiving Jacob. I can see he is a good man. I don't want to carry this anger anymore. Please help me.

The evening before hadn't been torture. She wouldn't have thought that possible until recently. But she had seen a side of Jacob—even if they didn't agree about Andy and Lisa—which she liked. He cared about the children at the refuge. He cared about his patients. He cared about his friends.

If Jacob could move past Kevin's death, then so could she. She would find a way because she wanted to continue working at the refuge and that meant being involved with him.

"We need to stop meeting like this," Jacob said several weeks later as he closed the door to the exam room.

Hannah held Nancy in her lap, the child's head lying on her shoulder. "Just as soon as they come up with a cure for the common cold and a few other illnesses."

He knelt next to Hannah. "What's wrong, Nancy?"

"I don't feel good."

He leaned closer to hear the weak answer. "Let's take your temperature first."

While he rose, Nancy's eyes grew round. "I don't want a shot."

Hannah cradled the child against her. "I gave her something for her fever last night, but she didn't sleep well. She ended up in my bed. She complained her throat hurts."

"Nancy, can you hop up here and let me take a look?" Jacob patted the exam table.

The little girl nodded, then slipped off Hannah's lap. Jacob helped her up, then placed a digital thermometer into her ear.

Hannah stood next to Nancy. "What is it now?"

"Hundred and four. When was the last time you gave her something for her fever?"

Hannah checked her watch. "Four hours ago."

When the nurse came into the room, Jacob examined the child, then took a swab of her throat. "Strep is going around. We should know something in a few minutes."

He handed the sample to Teresa, who left, then shook out two children's pain relievers and gave them to Nancy. After chewing them, she sipped the cup of water Jacob filled for her.

"If it's strep, you'll need to keep her away from the other children. It can be very contagious. I often see it make the rounds in a family." Jacob jotted something on the girl's chart.

"I'll have her stay in my room, but she ate dinner and breakfast with the whole crew."

"I'll give you a maintenance dose of antibiotics. I don't want you getting sick, too."

The door opened as Nancy leaned against Hannah as if the child didn't have the strength to keep herself upright. Teresa entered and handed Jacob a slip of paper.

He frowned. "It's strep." He scribbled on a prescription pad, then ripped it off and handed it to Hannah. "Get her started on that right away. I'll come by this evening to check the rest of the kids, as well, and see how Nancy is doing after she's had a dose of antibiotics and lots of rest. I'll bring maintenance doses for the children to take when they get home from school." He smoothed the child's hair from her face. "You'll rest for me, Nancy?"

She nodded and buried herself even more against Hannah.

"Great. I bet Teresa has a toy for you from the box. Do you want one?" Jacob sent his nurse a silent message.

Nancy's dull gaze slid from Jacob to the nurse. "Yes, please."

"What would you like?" Teresa took the child's hand and assisted her down from the exam table. "We've got some coloring books. Do you like to color?"

"Uh-huh."

"Then you can pick from several different ones." Teresa left the room with Nancy in tow.

The second they were gone, Hannah rounded on Jacob. "What didn't you say in front of Nancy?"

"This could be serious. Both Terry and Susie get strep throat easily. Last time Terry was very sick from it. I'll be there not long after they get home from school. Has Nancy been around them much, other than at dinner and breakfast?"

"Susie read to her last night. She's the one who came and told me Nancy wasn't feeling well and was hot." Hannah pictured the children all in bed with sore throats and fevers. "So do you think I'd better dust off my tennis shoes and get ready to run between bedrooms?"

He chuckled. "That's a possibility, but I'll help as much as I can."

The barrier around her heart crumpled a little as she looked into his eyes. Since he'd come into her life, he was doing that a lot—helping her out.

Hannah collapsed onto the couch in the living area and rested her head on the back cushion. "Thankfully Terry doesn't have strep yet, but I'm worried about Susie."

"I've got her on an antibiotic. We caught it early this time so she should be all right in a few days." Jacob settled across from her in a lounge chair.

"Are you as tired as I am?"

"I could fall asleep sitting up in this chair."

"Are you going to be all right driving home?"

One corner of his mouth lifted. "Sure, if I can persuade you to fix me a cup of coffee."

"Won't that keep you up after you get home?"

"I'm just hoping it will keep me up *until* I get home."

"If you think there'll be a problem, you are welcome to stay here and sleep on this couch." She patted the black leather cushion.

"No. My new car practically drives itself."

Summoning her last bit of energy, Hannah pushed to her feet. "One cup of java coming up then."

In the kitchen she quickly brewed some coffee, amazed that she actually invited him to stay over. It wasn't as though they would be alone, not with eight children in the house—six of them sick and probably up and down the whole night until the antibiotic really took effect.

But a picture of his tired face popped into her mind as she stared at the dark liquid dripping into the pot. It was after one, and he'd spent over nine hours here, helping her with the children—and that was after working a full day at his office. With Meg off, she'd needed the help, and she hadn't wanted to expose anyone else to strep.

Thank You, Lord, for sending him to us.

The aroma of coffee permeated the kitchen, tempting her to drink a cup herself. But she needed to get what rest she could so she only filled a mug for Jacob, then walked back into the living room to find him sound asleep. Even in relaxation he appeared exhausted, his pale features highlighting the dark circles under his eyes.

After placing his coffee on the table beside his chair, she grabbed the coverlet from the couch and threw it over him, pausing for a long moment to stare at him. Until she realized what she was doing. Quickly she dimmed the lights and tiptoed out of the living area. On her way to her bedroom, she checked on the children. The sick kids were separated from the two who were still healthy and she hoped stayed that way.

All seemed well as she headed for her room and bed. She was so tired she didn't even bother removing her clothes. She plopped down on the bedspread and fell back onto the pillow. The softness cocooned her in luxury that her weary body craved.

A thought seeped into her mind. She needed to get up and take her maintenance dose. She'd forgotten earlier. She would…soon….

The next thing Hannah knew someone was shaking her arm. She popped one eye open to find Nancy by her bed, her thumb in her mouth, her face flushed. "Baby, what's wrong?" She pushed herself up on her elbows.

"I can't sleep," she mumbled with her thumb still in her mouth.

Hannah touched her forehead, then cupped her cheek. Fever radiated beneath her palm. She slid her glance to the clock. Four. She'd slept almost three hours. "Let me give you some more pain reliever."

Hannah hurried into the bathroom off her room and retrieved the medicine and a paper cup full of water. When she returned, she found Nancy curled on her bed, still sucking her thumb. "Here, chew these first then drink some water."

Nancy did, then lay back down, her movements lethargic.

"I'll carry you to your room."

"Not mine. It's Susie's. Can I stay here?"

Hannah pulled a chair near the bed and sat. "Okay. This time. I'll take you…"

The child's eyes drifted closed. She'd wait until Nancy was asleep then take her back to the bedroom she shared with the two other girls. Fifteen minutes later she scooped up Nancy into her arms and strode out into the hallway and nearly collided with Jacob, who held Andy against him.

"What happened?" Hannah stepped back.

"He's sick, too. He woke me up in the living room."

"That makes seven now."

"Put him in my bed. I don't want him going back into the room with Terry."

Jacob passed her and entered her bedroom while she quickly took care of Nancy. She tucked the little girl in and brushed her fingers along her forehead. Her skin was cooler to the touch. Relief flowed through Hannah as she checked on the other two girls then slipped out into the hallway. Hopefully by this evening the children would be much better with no complications from the strep.

When Jacob came out of her room, she asked, "Are you hungry? I'll fix you an early breakfast or a late-night snack, whichever way you want to look at it."

"I never turn down a chance at a meal I don't have to fix. And after the past—" he glanced at his watch "—twelve hours I'm starved."

As she made her way to the kitchen, the hairs on her nape tingled as though Jacob was staring at her. She didn't dare look back to see if he was. Just thinking about it caused her cheeks to flame.

After flipping on the light, she crossed the room, opened the refrigerator and removed ingredients for scrambled eggs. "Frankly I love having breakfast at any time of the day. Mom used to fix pancakes for dinner once a month."

When he didn't say anything, she peered back at him. A shadow dulled his eyes until he saw her staring and a veil descended over his expression.

He moved to her. "Can I help?"

"Someone who professes not to cook? I don't think so. Have a seat. This is the least I can do for all your help with the kids."

"I'm their doctor."

"Who's gone above and beyond the call of duty."

He scooted back a chair from the kitchen table and sank down onto it. His gaze captured hers and for a moment she forgot everything but the charming smile that tilted the corners of his mouth and the gleam that sparkled in his eyes.

She blinked and he looked away. She quickly turned back to the counter, found a mixing bowl and began cracking eggs into it. "What made you become a doctor?"

A good minute passed before he answered, "I wanted to heal."

The anguish that slipped through his words froze Hannah. Heal himself? Or heal others? Suddenly she remembered anew who was sitting a few feet away from her. For a while she'd forgotten that he'd been responsible for her brother's death. Her hand trembled so badly she had to grip the edge of the counter.

"Hannah, are you all right?"

The sound of the chair scraping across the tile floor focused her on the here and now. Jacob had asked a question. She needed to answer him. She cleared her throat and said, "I'm just tired and concerned about the kids."

"They're a tough bunch. I think we caught it early." He stood right behind her.

His presence electrified the air. *Lord, help me to forgive. How did You do it on the cross?*

"Are you sure I can't help?"

Fortifying her defenses, she swung around and took a step back. "Yes, I'm sure. You're my guest. Now, sit and behave." She needed him across the room. She needed some space while she mended her composure, and it was hard to think straight with him so near.

He held up his hands. "Okay. I'm going." After he resettled in the chair, he asked, "Has being a social worker been everything you wanted it to be?"

That was an easy question thankfully. She turned back to finish preparing the scrambled eggs. "Yes, I love kids and wanted to make a difference in their lives, but I couldn't see myself as a teacher." She poured the mixture into the heated skillet. "I like a challenge, and I think social work is definitely challenging."

"That's putting it mildly."

She stirred the eggs. "I would think being a doctor is one, too."

"I guess you and I are alike. I enjoy a good challenge. It keeps life interesting."

The third thing they had in common. At this rate there would be no differences between them. After sticking four pieces of bread into the toaster, she withdrew some dishes from the cabinet and brought them to the table.

Before she went back to the stove to get the food, Jacob caught her hand and held it, drawing her full attention to his handsome face. "Thank you for covering me with a blanket." His voice dropped a level, a huskiness in it.

His hand about hers, warm and strong, robbed her of words. For the life of her, she couldn't look away, as though his eyes lured her into their brown depths. "You're welcome," she managed to say, her mouth parched.

The silence grew until she thought he must hear her heart pounding. All she could remember was his dedication to helping the children the evening before. A connection between them sprang up that staggered Hannah, a connection that went beyond what they had in common.

Finally he released her grasp. A smile dimpled his cheeks. "You'd better get the eggs."

She spun around and hurried to the stove, gripping the wooden spoon and counter to keep her hands from quivering. What just happened? How could she betray her brother's memory like that? It was one thing to forgive—but to forget? No!

While she saved the breakfast from being ruined, she tried to bring her rebellious emotions under control. It was because she was so exhausted, she told herself, that for a moment she looked beyond what Jacob had done in the past to what he was doing in the present.

Chapter Seven

Hannah sat at the kitchen table, trying to drink a cup of warm milk to help her sleep. It curdled her stomach. She pushed it away and buried her face in her hands. Fever singed her palms. Her throat burned. She didn't need a doctor to tell her that after a day and a half taking care of the sick children, she'd caught what they had. Thankfully most of them were on the mend, except Terry who had come down with it earlier today. Jacob didn't think the boy would have it too badly since he'd already taken two doses of the maintenance antibiotic. Up until an hour ago when she began to feel sick, she'd forgotten to take hers. Obviously she was too late to prevent it totally.

The sound of the door opening alerted Hannah she wasn't alone. Dropping her hands onto the table, she straightened as Meg came into the room.

"Everyone's in bed. Anything else you need before I go home?" Meg stopped near her, her eyes narrowing on Hannah. "You've got a rash, Hannah!"

"A rash?"

"All over your face and neck."

Hannah glanced down as though she could see it in the surface of the table.

The older woman touched Hannah's forehead. "You've got a fever. Come on. You're going to bed now." She took her arm to help Hannah rise.

She tried to stand and swayed. The room spun. "But the kids need—"

"I'll take care of the children. Don't you worry." Meg supported most of Hannah's weight as she headed toward the bedroom area.

"But you might get sick, too."

"If I do, then I'll deal with it. Right now you worry about taking care of yourself. I wonder why the maintenance dose didn't work for you. You've been on it for a while."

"I forgot until an hour ago. I was too busy taking care of the others."

Meg flipped back the coverlet and helped Hannah ease down onto her bed. "I'll get you some aspirin."

Hannah slid her eyes closed, listening to Meg move about the room, the sound loud to her sensitive ears. Her face felt on fire. Pain gripped her throat and drummed against her skull.

"Here." Meg slipped her arm underneath Hannah and lifted her up to take the pills and drink some water.

The second Hannah managed to swallow the aspirin she sagged back onto the mattress, shutting her eyes to the swirling room.

As the pain continued to do a tap dance in her head, she embraced the darkness.

"Why didn't she say anything to me before I left this evening?" Jacob stared at Hannah sleeping fitfully on her bed.

"I don't think she was thinking about herself. She's got a bad rash," Meg said.

The tiny red spots stood out like a neon sign against the otherwise pale skin. He brushed back a strand of hair from her face, feeling the warmth beneath his fingertips. "That can happen sometimes with strep. I'm going to give her a shot." He opened his medicine bag and took out a syringe and a vial of antibiotics. "I hate to wake her up, but she needs this now."

"I'm staying tonight to make sure the children are taken care of. You take care of her." Meg crossed to the door and left.

Gently, he shook Hannah awake. Her eyes blinked, then drifted closed.

"Hannah, I need to know if you're allergic to any medicine."

"Medicine?" she mumbled.

"I want to give you a shot of an antibiotic."

Her eyes popped open and focused on him. "A shot? I hate them."

Jacob pulled a chair close to the bed and sat.

"I'm worried about you. Are you allergic to anything?"

"No—you don't need to worry…" Her voice floated into the silence as she surrendered to sleep again.

She flinched when the needle pricked her skin, but her eyes stayed closed. Again he combed the wayward lock back from her forehead, then went to the living room to settle into a chair for the long night ahead. He wouldn't leave until he was sure she would be all right.

Hannah moaned. Every muscle ached. She tried to turn over onto her side, but someone held her hand. Easing one eye open, she stared at Jacob stretched out in a chair next to her bed, asleep. She tugged herself free at the same time he snapped upright, disoriented. His hair lay at odd angles, making him appear younger.

He chuckled. "I guess you caught me napping on the job."

Her mind still shrouded in a fog, she mumbled, "What job?"

He bent forward, taking her wrist and placing his fingers over her pulse. "Caring for you."

She struggled to sit up. "I don't need you…" She collapsed back onto the pillow.

"What were you saying?"

She inhaled a shallow, raspy breath. "I'll be fine with some rest." She shifted her head until she glimpsed her clock on the bedside table. "I've only been sleeping a few hours…" The light slanting through the slits in the blinds attracted her attention. "What time of day is it?"

"It's eleven in the morning."

"I slept all night?" Again she tried to sit up and managed to prop herself on her elbows. "What about the children?"

"Meg has been here taking care of them. I've looked in on each one, and all of them are recovering nicely. And there were no cases at the other cottage."

"What about your patients?"

His chuckles evolved into laughter. "I know I work a lot, but today is Saturday. I'd planned to spend it here making sure the kids were all right."

"You were? I mean, I don't remember…." She rubbed her temple, the pounding in her head less but still there. She swallowed several times to coat her dry throat. "Can I have some water?"

"Sure." He rose and settled next to her to hold her up while she sipped some cold liquid. Despite its coolness, it burned going down. "I need you to take these." Jacob produced some pills. "And there's no forgetting this time."

She winced each time one went down. "I guess I forgot to tell you I used to get strep throat every year while growing up."

"No, you left that out."

"It wouldn't have made any difference. I'd still have taken care of the children. They needed me." The sound of her voice grew weak in her ears.

Jacob laid her gently back on the bed and stood.

"Somehow I figured that. But now I'm your doctor, and I'm telling you to sleep and not worry about anything."

"You're a pediatrician." Her eyes fluttered closed.

"But I'm free and here. You aren't going to get rid of me."

That last sentence comforted her as sleep descended.

"She's awake, Dr. Jacob! She's awake!"

Nancy's shrieking voice thundered through Hannah's head, threatening to renew the earlier hammering pain.

"Shh." Jacob filled the doorway with several children standing behind him, peeping into the room.

He looked good to her tired eyes. Very good. Slightly worn but handsome as ever with his tousled brown hair and gleaming eyes that held hers. "How long have I been asleep?"

"It's Sunday afternoon and Laura and Peter are here."

"I lost another day."

Nancy appeared in her face. "I was worried about you."

Other than the ashen cast to the little girl's features, she looked all right. The dullness in her eyes was gone and a smile brightened her face. "I'll be as good as new in a day or so."

"Okay, everyone, Laura and Peter have dished up some ice cream for you in the kitchen. You'd better eat it before it melts."

The sound of running footsteps faded down the hall, leaving Jacob alone with her. He moved into the room.

"I have news for you, Hannah. You won't be up and about in a day or so. You had a bad case of strep on top of exhaustion. You need to get a lot of rest if you want to be as good as new by Thanksgiving."

She frowned. "You aren't going to be one of these demanding doctors who insists I follow your instructions."

He stood with his feet slightly apart and his hands on his hips, glaring at her. "Yes, I am." But the merriment in his eyes mocked his fierce stance. "I came close to taking you to the hospital."

"You did?"

The implication threw her. If her aching body was any indication, she realized she had been very sick. But the hospital?

"Oh, you are awake? The kids said you were." Laura walked to the bed and positioned herself on the other side of Jacob. "I brought you some ice cream." She held up the bowl.

"Vanilla?"

Nodding, Laura sat in the chair nearby and scooped a spoonful of it for Hannah. "Peter could use your help, Jacob. By now all eight children are clamoring for more ice cream."

"Make sure she stays in bed," was his parting remark.

Laura laughed. "He can be so demanding when a patient doesn't follow his instructions."

Hannah scooted up against the headboard and took the bowl from Laura. "This does make me realize I have to find a doctor. I haven't yet."

Laura's laughter increased. "Jacob has a way with children, but I can see his bedside manner might be lacking with an adult. He does mean well, though."

Hannah slid the spoonful of ice cream into her mouth and relished the coldness as she swallowed the treat. "I wouldn't know about his bedside manner. I was pretty out of it. I remember him making me take some pills, though."

Laura's expression sobered. "Yes, I know. Peter and I have been here helping Meg with the children. You should have let us know how bad it was. We could have come sooner."

Hannah stared at her ice cream. "You have four children. I didn't want you to be exposed to strep, so I played it down when we talked."

"And got Meg and Jacob to go along."

"I thought we were handling it. We did. I just got sick."

"Running yourself into the ground. In fact, I tried to get Jacob to go home and take care of himself, but he wouldn't leave your side."

"He didn't?" Warmth, that had nothing to do with a fever, spread through her.

"He told me he wouldn't be able to sleep until he knew you were out of the woods. For the past day and a half he has stood guard over you." Laura glanced toward the doorway. "Now, I'm gonna insist he go home and get some rest."

Hannah took another scoop of the ice cream. "Do we have any Popsicle treats left?"

"You must be getting better. You have an appetite. I'll see if I can find any. The children have been eating them right and left. I had Peter go get some more." She rose and headed for the hallway.

Hannah finished her treat and placed the bowl on the table, tired from the brief exertion. How was she going to look after eight children? She couldn't even feed herself without getting exhausted.

She tried to concentrate on that dilemma, but she kept thinking about what Laura had told her about Jacob. He hadn't left her side. He'd watched over her. She should be upset by that news, but after the past few days working with him to take care of the sick children, she wasn't. A bond of friendship had formed between them.

Lord, if any good has come out of the illness that took hold of this house, it was that. I don't hate Jacob anymore. I can forgive him for what happened to Kevin. The man I've gotten to know would never have done something like that on purpose. The car wreck was an unfortunate accident that I suspect has left a mark on Jacob, too.

She sank farther into her pillow, propped up against the headboard, and closed her eyes. Total peace blanketed her for the first time in years. *This is why you forgive someone. This is why you let go of your anger. I understand now, Jesus, why You forgave them on the cross. Thank You, Lord.*

Footsteps announced she wasn't alone. She

opened her eyes, expecting to see Laura, but instead Jacob entered with a cherry Popsicle in his grasp.

"I hear you're hungry." He sat in the chair by the bed and gave her the treat.

"I thought Laura was making you go home to sleep."

"She tried."

"And obviously failed."

"I can be a very determined man."

"I appreciate all you've done, but she's right. I don't want you to get sick, too." She nibbled on her Popsicle.

"I'm not going to. I've built up quite a resistance. Remember I deal with sick kids all the time."

"Now I see why the children love having you come. The gifts you brought them to keep them occupied and in bed were great."

"I love those handheld video games."

"You sound like you've played your share of them."

"I'm a kid at heart."

His smile encompassed his whole face and sent her heart beating a shade faster. "I'll have to try one sometime."

"I'll loan you one of mine. A great stress reliever."

"I thought exercise was."

"I'm exercising my mind."

Seeing his well-proportioned body, she knew he also had to exercise physically, too. "I like to ride my bike but haven't had a chance yet."

"There are some great places around here to

visit. If the weather stays nice, I could show you one weekend."

"You have a bike?"

He nodded. "A great stress reliever."

"Maybe I could get some bikes for the kids, and we could all go on an excursion one Saturday."

"Let's get you well first, then we can plan something."

"I'll be up in no time." She fluttered her hand in the air, but immediately dropped it into her lap, her arm feeling as though it weighed more than a twenty-pound barbell.

He rose. "I'd better let you get some rest. Besides, I promised Laura I would deliver the Popsicle and leave. I don't want to make a liar out of me."

The second he left, Hannah felt the energy level in the room diminish. He charged the air wherever he was. He had a presence about him that drew a person to him. Why hadn't she noticed that before?

Because I had been too busy trying to avoid him.

It was nice having a friend in Cimarron City.

A friend? a little voice questioned.

Yes, a friend. Anything else would be taking this forgiveness thing too far.

"Dr. Jacob has pulled up," Gabe shouted from the window in the living room.

"Mom's here!" Andy jumped up and down, then raced for the front door.

Hannah laughed. "I think he's excited."

"He's been marking off his calendar until Thanksgiving." Susie followed Andy outside.

Hannah heard the car doors slamming shut. She hurried after the children who flooded out of the house and down the steps. Excitement bubbled up in her. She wished she could attribute it totally to the fact that Lisa had just finished her drug-rehab program and was going to join them for Thanksgiving dinner today. She couldn't, though. After she was up and about at the end of last week, she hadn't seen much of Jacob other than at church on Sunday. But today he was spending Thanksgiving with them.

Whenever he was at the cottage, it seemed to come alive. His relationship with the children was great.

How about his with you?

She ignored the question and greeted Lisa with a hug. "It's good to see you."

The young woman slung her arm around Andy who was plastered against his mom. "Thanks for the invitation. I've been looking forward to today."

Andy yanked on his mother's arm. "Come inside. I want to show you what Dr. Jacob got me."

"I'll show you my gift, too," Gabe said.

"Talk to you later," Lisa said laughingly as her son dragged her up the steps and into the house.

Hannah turned to Jacob. "I appreciate you picking her up."

"No problem. I was coming this way." He produced a bouquet of fall flowers from behind his back. "These are for you."

"Me?" She took them, her eyes probably as round as the yellow mums she held. The scent of the lilies teased her senses.

"Dr. Jacob, have you heard about the bike trip we're going on this weekend?" Nancy asked, tugging on his arm to get his attention.

He knelt down so that they were eye to eye. "I'm going, too."

"Oh, yeah. I forgot." The little girl hugged her worn pink blanket to her and stuck her thumb into her mouth.

"C'mon, Nancy. You need to help me set the table." Susie clasped the child's hand and mounted the steps. "Where are the other kids?"

Still stunned by the gesture, Hannah was momentarily speechless. She could not recall anyone ever bringing her flowers—not even her husband.

"Hannah?"

"Oh. At the barn feeding the animals. They'll be here shortly. Roman took several of them over with some of the older kids."

"I bet Terry led the way."

"You know that boy well."

"He has been here the longest. I wish someone would adopt him, but he's nearly twelve, which makes it harder." Jacob held the front door open for Hannah.

"Yeah, everyone wants a baby or a young child when they're looking to adopt."

The aroma of the roasting turkey seeped into every corner of the house. "Ah, the best smell. Did Meg make her cornbread dressing?"

"Yes, and my contribution is dessert. Pecan pie."

"A woman after my heart. That's one of my favorite desserts."

"Meg made her pumpkin pie and a chocolate one, too."

"Stop right there. You're driving a starving man crazy."

"Tell you what. Dinner isn't for another hour. Let me put these flowers into water and check with the kids to see if anyone wants to go to the barn. That oughta take your mind off food."

"Great. If I stayed here, I'd probably be raiding the kitchen, and Meg doesn't take too kindly to snacking before a meal."

She waved her hand toward the living room. "Two are in there. See if they want to go," she said while she walked to the dining room and peered in.

Susie gave Nancy a plate to set on the table.

"Want to come to the barn with Dr. Jacob and me?"

Nancy thrust the dishes she still held at Susie. "Yes!"

The older girl scanned the near-empty table. "I promised Meg I would help her. You all go on without me."

Next Hannah found Gabe and Andy in the boys' bedroom, showing Lisa how to play one of the handheld video games. "We're going to the barn. Want to come?"

Gabe leaped to his feet at the same time Andy did. The boy pulled his mother up.

"I guess that's a yes," Hannah said, and went to

the kitchen to let Meg know where they would be and put the flowers in water.

Five minutes later the group passed the unfinished third house and started hiking across the meadow. With just a hint of crispness, the air felt nice. The scent of burning wood lingered on the light breeze that blew a few strands of Hannah's hair across her face. Andy practically hauled Lisa behind him at a fast clip while the other children ran and skipped toward the red barn.

"After the busy week I've had, I don't have that kind of energy." Jacob chuckled when Andy's mother threw them a helpless look.

"Do you think Lisa will be successful this time?"

"Honestly? No, I don't but then my experience hasn't been a good one when it comes to successful stories with drug rehab."

"I'm praying you're wrong."

Jacob paused in the middle of the field and looked long and hard at Hannah. "Truthfully I hope I am, too."

The more she was around Jacob, the more she realized she'd never met a man like him. He was honest, caring, and when he was wrong, admitted it. If she weren't careful, she would forget who he was. Yes, she had forgiven him, but she hadn't forgotten what happened all those years ago. To do so would have been to betray her family.

Peter came out of the barn as the children with Lisa raced by him. "The kids are almost through feeding the animals." He swung his attention from

Hannah to Jacob. "Now I know why you turned Laura and me down for Thanksgiving dinner. The kids told me you were joining them today."

"I got an offer I couldn't refuse." Jacob's grin accentuated his two dimples.

"Laura and I will eventually get over it." Peter shifted toward Hannah. "I hope you have enough food. You should have seen him last Thanksgiving."

"Hannah, look." Nancy walked toward her with a puppy cradled against her chest. "I got to pick her up this time."

"Yeah, she's just about ready for a home." Peter started for the interior of the barn.

"I can give her a home," Nancy said, trailing after Peter with the mutt still in her arms. "I'm good with puppies."

"So far I've managed to discourage any pets at the cottage, but I've got my work cut out for me this time." Hannah hurried to follow Nancy.

"Why? I think a pet around the house would be good for the kids."

She stopped in the middle of the cavernous building. "And how do you suppose I should pick the pet? Each child wants a different one."

Jacob scratched the top of his head. "I don't know. I'll have to think on that one."

"Fine. You come up with a fair way and they can have one."

Terry entered through the back door, carrying a lamb. "I found him." He passed the animal to

Peter, then waved at Hannah. "I'm finished. Is it time for dinner?"

"About half an hour." Hannah swung her attention back to Nancy and saw the little girl put the white puppy back in its pen with the other ones. The child stooped down and continued to stroke the mutt.

Jacob was right. There needed to be some pets at the cottage, not just down at the barn. She'd never gotten to have one because they had always been moving to a new place. She remembered her yearning and her promise to herself that when she had her own home she would have several to make up for the lack while growing up.

"I've got it." Jacob leaned close, his voice low. "Paul used to have a family meeting every week and everyone had an equal say in what was discussed. That's where we often hashed out problems that came up. When something like having a pet needed to be decided upon, we would talk about it at the meeting, then vote. Majority ruled."

His warm breath tingled along her neck. She stepped a few feet away and tried to slow her suddenly pounding heart. "That might work."

"He set up ground rules. One person at a time spoke. No one was allowed to cut in until that person was through speaking. Everyone had to be respectful of the others. Our voting was done by secret balloting and no one was to be questioned how they voted."

"He sounds like an amazing man."

"He was. I miss him. Thankfully Alice, his wife, lives with Laura and Peter."

"Alice was your foster mother? I didn't know that." She'd met the older woman while visiting Laura once.

"Yes. Both of them were lifesavers to a lot of kids."

"Including you?"

"Especially me. I was pretty messed up when I went to live with the Hendersons at fifteen."

"Why?"

A frown marred his face and his eyes darkened with storm clouds.

Hannah wished she could snatch the question back. Would he say anything about the wreck? Was that even what he was referring to?

Chapter Eight

For a few seconds the urge to share inundated Jacob. He'd never told anyone but Paul. Jacob stared into her gaze, void of any judgment. The words formed in his mind.

"Jacob?"

He turned away from Hannah in the middle of the barn and strode to the entrance. How could he tell her what he'd done, that he'd been responsible for another person's death? He valued her friendship and didn't want to see disappointment, or something worse, in her eyes. Their rocky start had finally smoothed out. He didn't want to go back to how it had been in the beginning.

Hannah's hand settled on his arm. The touch went straight to his heart. The guilt he'd lived with for twenty-one years whisked the words away. He couldn't tell her, but he had to say something.

He glanced at her slightly behind him and to the

side. "Before I came to the Hendersons, I was an angry teen who had even run away from several foster homes."

"Because of your childhood?" Sympathy edged her voice.

"Yes. Paul's the one who taught me about Jesus. He showed me there was another way besides giving in to my anger."

"Anger can consume a person."

"It nearly had me. I never want to go back to that place." He shuddered.

Hannah moved to stand in front of Jacob. Her fingers skimmed down his arm, and she grasped his hand. "I don't see that happening."

"Not as long as the Lord is in my life."

"Hannah, I'm finished. I forgot to eat breakfast," Terry said.

She looked beyond Jacob and grinned. "Gather the others and we'll head back."

In the past few years he'd done a pretty good job of throwing himself totally into his work and putting the past behind him. But lately he hadn't been able to do that. *Why, Lord? Why now?*

Nancy took his hand. "I don't want to leave Abby."

"Abby?" That was Nancy's mother's name.

She pointed toward the pen. "The puppy. I named her Abby. I love that name."

His heart ripped in half, and he had no words for Nancy, having been in her shoes and remembering the pain of rejection he'd suffered as a child. Racking his brain for something to say, Jacob cleared his throat. "I like the name, too."

Nancy tugged him down and whispered in his ear, "Will you talk to Hannah about Abby?"

A lump lodged in his throat. "Sure."

Hannah sat at one end of the long dining-room table with Jacob at the other end. For the past minute silence had ruled because all the children were stuffing bites of pie into their mouths.

Jacob pushed his empty plate away. "That's it. I'm full up to my earlobes. Any more and it will come out the top of my head."

A couple of the children giggled.

"Dr. Jacob, you're funny," Nancy said, shoving her plate away. "I'm full up to my earlobes, too."

"That was the best Thanksgiving dinner I've had, Meg." Jacob wiped his mouth with his napkin.

The older woman blushed. "Oh, it was nothing."

"Who agrees with me?"

Everyone's arm shot up into the air. Meg beamed from ear to ear.

"And to show my appreciation, I'll clean up the dishes. Who's going to help me?" Jacob scanned the children's faces.

Everyone's arm dropped.

Hannah fought to keep her expression serious. "I guess you're stuck doing them by yourself."

"Who's going to take pity on me and help?" Jacob's gaze again flitted from one child to the next.

"I will," Lisa said.

"I can." Andy stood and gathered up his plate.

"Thanks, you two, but you enjoy your time together. I'll help Dr. Jacob." Hannah rose.

Before she had a chance to reach for the dishes in front of her, the children fled the dining room with Lisa and Meg following at a more sedate pace.

"I've never seen them move quite so fast," Jacob said with a chuckle.

"Not cleaning up is quite a motivator."

"Wash or dry?"

"You're the guest. You choose." She stacked the plates and carried them into the kitchen.

Five minutes later with the table cleared, Jacob rolled up his long sleeves and began rinsing the dishes off for the dishwasher. "Noah said something about coming over after eating at Peter and Laura's."

"Speaking of Noah, I've been thinking. Do you think he'll give Lisa a job at one of his restaurants?"

"You'll have to ask him. He's always looking for good help. Why? Did Lisa say something to you?"

"Well, no, but she doesn't have a job. I thought I would help her find something."

"Don't you think you should talk to her first?"

Hannah took the glass that Jacob handed her. "I didn't want to get her hopes up if it wasn't possible. She doesn't have many skills and has only worked in a fast-food restaurant."

"It'll be hard finding a decent job without a high-school diploma. Will she be able to stay at the halfway house?"

"Yes, and they have a program there that assists people in getting their GED."

Jacob shifted to face her. "Hannah, you can't live Lisa's life for her. She has to want it—especially being off drugs—if it's going to work."

She averted her gaze, uncomfortable under the intensity of his. "I know. She loves Andy. I know it. They belong together."

"Then she'll stay off the drugs if that's the way to be involved in his life." Sharpness sliced through his words.

Reestablishing eye contact with him, she glimpsed the pain he experienced as a child who hadn't meant much to his mother—at least not enough to stop taking drugs. "I have to try to help. That's why I went into social work in the first place." She took another dish from him. "In fact, I found Nancy's mother. She's only thirty miles from here in Deerfield."

He arched a brow. "And what do you intend to do with that information?"

"I'm going to see her next Wednesday."

"Do you want some company?"

Surprised, she immediately answered, "Yes," then took a harder look at Jacob and noticed the tightening about his mouth and the inflexibility in his eyes. "Why do you want to come?"

"I don't want you to go alone. I've read Nancy's file. I know the rough characters her mother has hung out with." Censorship sounded in his voice.

Hannah straightened, thrusting back her shoulders. "I have to try. Have you seen how upset Nancy is when she sees Andy with his mother?"

"Yes, I've seen her carrying her blanket and sucking her thumb more and more since Lisa has come into Andy's life."

"She misses her own mother."

"Maybe. But maybe she's just plain scared her mother might come get her."

"I don't think so. She's asked me tons of questions about my mother."

Mouth tightening, Jacob squirted some detergent into the sink and filled it up with hot water. "What time did you want to go? I can rearrange my afternoon appointments if that's okay with you."

"Fine. How about after lunch?"

"How about lunch then we can go?"

"Lunch?"

His chuckle tingled down her spine. "Yes, you've got to eat. I've got to eat. Let's do it together then leave from there."

"Sure."

"Then it's a date."

A date? No, it wasn't a date, she wanted to shout, but realized her panic would be conveyed. Instead she clamped her teeth together and didn't say another thing until they had finished up with the pots and pans.

While she put away the meat platter, Jacob wiped down the counters. "Does Nancy's mother know you're coming?"

Jacob's question in the quiet startled her. She whirled around. "No, I thought I would surprise her."

"I hope you're not the one who is surprised."

She frowned. "I'm not totally naive. I don't expect the woman to welcome me with open arms."

"That's good because she won't."

Tension pulsated between them as he stared at her.

Terry burst into the kitchen. "Noah is here! You've got to come see what he brought us." The boy spun around and disappeared back through the entrance.

"Was that Terry who blew in and out of here?" Hannah asked with a laugh, needing to change the subject.

"Yep."

The huge grin on Jacob's face prompted her to ask, "Do you know what Noah brought?"

He nodded and quickly followed the boy out of the kitchen.

Exasperated at the lack of information, Hannah left, too, and found all the children out front, surrounding a pickup filled with bicycles, many different sizes. She stopped at Jacob's side. "I guess that answers my problem about bikes for a ride. I'd only been able to come up with a few. Peter said he would work on it for me."

"He did. Noah and I were his solution."

"Y'all donated them?"

Jacob's smile grew. "Yep. It should have been done before now. Sometimes I'm so focused on their well-being physically that I forget about their mental health."

He waded his way through the crowd of children to help Noah lift the bikes out of the truck bed. As the two men did, they presented each one to a different kid.

Nancy hung back next to Hannah. The little girl glanced up at her. "I don't know how to ride. I've never had a bike."

Hannah pointed toward one still in the bed of the pickup. "That's why there are training wheels on that one. Before you know it, you'll be riding everywhere."

The child stared at it, doubt in her eyes, a tiny frown on her face. "I guess." She lowered her gaze to the ground at her feet.

"I'll work with you this afternoon since Dr. Jacob and I want to take all of you on a bike ride this Saturday. He said something about there being a small lake near here that we could go to and have a picnic. What do you think?"

"Can I bring Abby?"

Hannah knelt in front of Nancy. "A bike ride probably isn't the best place for a puppy."

Jacob approached the little girl. "Here's yours." He set Nancy's small bike with training wheels on it next to her.

She put her thumb in her mouth and looked up shyly at him, mumbling, "Thanks."

Hannah settled her hand on the child's shoulder. She saw the concern in Jacob's expression and said, "I'm going to teach her how to ride over the next two days. She never has."

Before he could say anything, the children encircled Noah and him, vying for the men's attention with their enthusiasm.

"Andy's always wanted a bike. He used to ride the boy's in the apartment across the hall." Lisa said, while watching her son, happiness plastering a smile on his face. "Who's that with Dr. Hartman?"

"Noah Maxwell. He owns the Pizzeria chain. In fact, I wanted to talk to you about applying for a job. Would you be interested in working at one of his restaurants? I could talk to him for you if you are." Jacob had been right—again. She needed to see if Lisa wanted a job at the Pizzeria before approaching Noah.

"At the halfway house they were going to help me look for something. 'Bout the only experience I have is at a food joint. One of the things I learnt at the rehab center was to ask for help when I need it. Thanks."

"Then I'll talk to Noah."

Andy ran up to his mom. "Dr. Jacob said I could go on a bike ride with them on Saturday because my cast is coming off tomorrow." After his announcement, he twirled around and raced back to the group.

Lisa followed her son, plowing into the middle of the children all getting on their bikes.

"Do you want to start your lesson now?" Hannah asked Nancy, who kept her gaze glued to the ground.

She shook her head. "I don't wanna go on a ride. Can I stay here?"

"Why, honey?" Hannah lifted the child's chin.

Tears pooled in Nancy's eyes, and several coursed down her cheeks. "I just don't. I heard Mommy say bikes are dangerous." The little girl pulled away and stepped back toward the porch. She plopped down on the top stair, sucking her thumb and hugging her blanket.

"Nancy doesn't want to ride?" Jacob stood right behind her.

"No. She thinks they're dangerous." Hannah kept her voice low so no one else heard.

"Having seen my share of bike accidents, I can't totally disagree, but we've also gotten helmets for them."

"I'll see if someone can watch her while we go with the other children. I don't want to force Nancy. Hopefully she'll see the others enjoying it and want to learn to ride."

Dressed in black slacks and a gray pullover sweater, Noah approached. "I think our gift is a big hit."

"Did you have any doubt?" Hannah scanned the smiling kids and wanted to bottle this moment.

"No. But what are we going to do for Christmas? It will be hard to top this."

"You don't have—"

"This is the best way I can spend my money," Noah interrupted Hannah. "These kids' lives have been hard. Giving them some joy is priceless."

She realized Noah had as big a heart as Jacob. Too bad, according to Laura, he didn't want to settle down and have his own family. "I do have a favor to ask."

"If it's to go on the bike ride, I draw the line there."

"No. I'd like you to interview Andy's mother for a job at your restaurant. She needs a job and the only experience she's had is as a waitress."

When she started to say more, Noah held up his hand. "Done. I'll talk to her."

Hannah was at a loss for words. Realizing Jacob's misgivings about Andy's mom wanting to change, she'd practiced her speech to convince Noah to give Lisa a chance.

"I'll give her a ride into town and talk to her tonight. Where's she staying?"

"She's staying at a halfway shelter two blocks from your first restaurant."

"Fine. I know where that is." There must have been something in her expression because he added, "I know she just completed a drug-rehab program. I'm aware of what goes on at the refuge even though I don't get to spend as much time out here as Jacob."

"Thanks. I appreciate you giving her a chance." When Noah joined a couple of the boys by his truck, she said to Jacob, "It's a shame he isn't interested in having a family. Like you, he's good with the kids."

"You think I'm good with them?" A gleam glinted in his gaze.

"We might not always see eye to eye on certain issues, but I can't ignore the fact you have a way with the children. Are you interested in having a family?" The second she asked the question she wanted to retreat. Why in the world had she asked him *that?* As if she might be interested in him and the answer.

"Yes. Paul was a great example of what a father can be."

"Then why don't you have one?" The urge to slap her hand over her mouth swamped her. She was digging a deep hole with her inquisitiveness.

He threw back his head and laughed. "I wish it were that simple. It takes two."

Heat flooded her cheeks. She started to mention he was thirty-five, but this time she managed to keep quiet. "Oh, look at Gabe ride."

On Saturday Hannah came to a stop near the small lake and hopped off her bicycle. Susie pulled up next to her while Jacob flanked her on the other side. "This is beautiful. We'll have to come back in the spring when the trees are flowering. I see quite a few redbuds."

"That's our state tree." Susie put her kickstand down. "We've been studying Oklahoma history in school."

"I can see why it is. They're everywhere."

"Can we walk along the shore? We won't go too far."

"Make sure no one goes too close to the water." Hannah took a swig from her water bottle.

"She told me Thanksgiving that she wanted to be

a doctor like me." After removing his ball cap, Jacob wiped his hand across his forehead. "I'd forgotten how much work bicycling is, especially that last hill."

"I thought you went bike riding all the time."

"When I was a child, I used to. I…" A frown carved deep lines into his brow.

"What?"

"My grandma gave me a bike one Christmas. I loved that bike. I would go all over the place. If I was quick enough, it became my way of escaping my mother when she went into a rage."

"What happened to it?"

"During one of my mother's rages, she ran over it with her car. I tried to fix it, but the frame was bent too much for me to do anything. I cried when the garbage man took it away." His gaze zeroed in on her. "That was the only time I cried. Not crying used to make my mom madder. She used to shout I didn't have a heart."

Her stomach knotted as she listened to him talk about his mother so dispassionately as though she were a stranger. But she'd gotten to know him well enough to hear the underlying pain that his words didn't reflect. "My mom and I had moved to a new town and I was desperate to impress the neighborhood kids." Hannah sipped some more cool water. "I performed a few tricks with my bike. They were properly awed until the last one. I fell and broke my wrist. I never got back on it after that. I stopped riding for years until college when I took it up for exercise."

"How did we get on a subject like this?"

"I don't know," she said with a shaky laugh.

"I know how." He shifted toward her. "I find it easy to talk to you. I don't tell others about my childhood. I prefer leaving that in my past."

His words made her feel special. Surprisingly she found it easy to talk to him, too. Less than two months ago she'd thought of him as her enemy. Now she considered him a friend—a very good friend.

He inched closer, taking her hands in his. "I haven't had much time in my life for dating. I made a promise years ago to become a doctor and that's where all my energy has gone."

Children's laughter drifted to her, reminding her they weren't alone. She peered at the group near the lake. Terry was showing Gabe how to skip rocks. Susie was scolding the two youngest boys to stay away from the water.

When she looked back at Jacob, the intensity in his gaze stole her breath. He bent toward her. Her heart fluttered in anticipation. He released her hands and cupped her face. He lowered his head until their mouths were inches apart. The scent of peppermint spiced the air.

Softly he brushed his lips across hers. "I think we should go out on an official date."

"You do?" she squeaked out, her pulse racing through her body.

"Don't you think we've skirted around this long enough?"

"What's this?"

His mouth grazed hers again. "This attraction between us."

She wanted his kiss. His eyes enticed her to forget who he was, to forget the past and grab hold of the future.

A drumroll blared. Hannah gasped and shot back.

Jacob's eyes widened. He stared at her pocket as another drumroll sounded, loud and demanding.

She dug into her jeans. "That's my cell."

"A drumroll? What kind of ring is that?"

She pulled the phone out. "One I know is mine." She flipped it open. "Hannah here."

"I'm so sorry to bother you."

The alarm in Meg's voice alerted Hannah something was wrong.

"Nancy's missing. I've looked everywhere and I can't find her."

Chapter Nine

Heart pounding, Hannah raced up the steps and into the cottage with Jacob and the children not far behind her. Meg stood in the living room with Peter, Laura, Roman and a police officer. The older woman reeled around when Hannah came in. The anxious look on Meg's face tightened a band about Hannah's chest. She gulped in deep breaths, but she couldn't seem to fill her lungs. Bending over, hands on knees, she inhaled over and over. She'd never ridden so fast before.

Meg touched Hannah's shoulder. "She's been gone for at least an hour. We've looked all over the farm, especially the barn."

"You didn't find her in the pen with the puppies? She's taken a liking to one of them."

Peter moved forward. "No, but now that I think about it, I didn't see all the puppies. At the time I thought one was behind its mama in the back."

"Is anything missing from her room?" Jacob strode in with the children.

Meg shook her head. "I don't think so, but I'm not that familiar with what she has." She snapped her fingers. "Except I know her blanket is gone. She had it with her while she was watching TV in here."

"I'll check her room. I know what she has." Hannah headed down the hallway, her hands shaking so badly she had to clasp them together.

She opened every drawer and the closet, then inspected under the bed and in Nancy's little toy chest. She finished her survey when Jacob appeared in the doorway.

"Anything?"

"Her doll she'd brought with her when she came to the cottage. I don't think she's been kidnapped. I think she's run away."

"Why? Where would she go?"

Her heartbeat pulsated against her eardrums. The constriction about her chest squeezed even tighter. "I don't know and tonight they are predicting it will drop below freezing with rain or snow."

"Let's hope they're wrong."

"Or we find her before then." Hannah welcomed Jacob's calming presence. She saw apprehension in his expression, but above everything his strength prevailed. He was a man used to emergencies and knew how to handle them.

Back in the living room the police officer tucked his notepad into his front pocket then peered at Hannah. "Anything else missing?"

"Her doll."

"I'll call this in and get things moving. Where's your phone?"

Meg pointed toward the kitchen. "I'll show you."

"We need to search the farm again." Jacob placed his arm about Hannah's shoulder. "Anywhere she really liked?"

"The barn."

"Well, let's start there and fan out."

"How about us?" Susie came forward with the other children, unusually quiet, standing behind her.

"We'll get Cathy and Roman to organize the children and search both cottages, the unfinished one and the surrounding area. Susie, you can help Cathy with the kids in our house." Seeing terror on a couple of their faces, Hannah added, "Nancy will be found. She'll be all right."

"Let's go next door where Cathy and the others are waiting." Roman led the way with the children following.

"I'll have Alexa and Sean meet us at the barn. They can help us search that area." Laura left with Peter.

Hannah started forward. Jacob's hand on her shoulder stopped her. She glanced back at him, such kindness in his eyes that tears welled up in hers. He drew her to him.

"We will find her and she will be all right."

His whispered words, raw with suppressed emotions, fueled her tears. Forcing them down, she backed away from the comfort of his arms. "I don't have time to cry. We only have a few hours before it gets dark."

Two hours later Hannah paused near the creek that ran through the farm. Thankfully it wasn't deep, the bottom easily seen. She peered at Jacob downstream from her. Fifteen minutes ago he found Nancy's doll by a bush where it appeared the little girl had sat. With that they were now concentrating on this area. Nancy had to be near. Nightfall would be in another hour.

"Nancy," Hannah shouted for the hundredth time, her voice raw. She heard the child's name from the others intermittently.

Hannah forged forward into the thicker underbrush, so glad it was too cold for snakes. But there were other animals that could do harm to a small child. Thinking about that possibility, she again yelled the girl's name and heard the frantic ring in her voice.

Only silence greeted her.

Her shoulders sagged as the minutes ticked away. She pushed farther into the wooded area, sending up another prayer for Nancy's safe return.

In the distance she saw a glimpse of pink. Hannah squinted and picked up her pace, although it was slower than usual because of the dense foliage.

"Nancy."

A sound caused her to stop and listen.

The breeze whistled through the forest. Disappointment cloaked her. *Just the wind.*

She continued toward the pink. The little girl's blanket was that color. "Nancy."

Another noise froze Hannah.

A whimper?

"Nancy, honey, where are you?"

Hannah kept moving forward, straining to hear anything unusual, trying to be as quiet as she could so she could listen.

"Hannah," a faint voice, full of tears, floated to her. From the direction of the pink.

"I'm coming."

Hannah tore through the brush, bare limbs clawing her. A branch scratched across her cheek. She fumbled for her cell in her pocket to alert the others she'd found Nancy. She hoped.

"Nancy, say something."

"I'm hurt."

The nearer she got to the pink the stronger the voice. She reached the blanket, but Nancy was nowhere to be seen.

"Honey, where are you? I don't see you."

"I'm down here."

Hannah stepped to the side several yards from the discarded blanket and looked down an incline. At the bottom lay Nancy with the puppy cuddled next to her, a ball of white fur.

"I see you. I'll be right there." Hannah flipped open her phone and punched in Jacob's number.

After giving him directions to where she thought she was, she started down the hill, half sliding as it got steeper toward the bottom. With a tearstained face, Nancy struggled to sit up and watched Hannah's descent. Abby began to yelp and prance around in circles.

When she reached the child, Nancy threw herself into Hannah's arms, sobbing. "You're okay now, honey."

She stroked the child's back, whispering she was safe over and over until Nancy finally calmed down and leaned back.

"Abby ran away from me. I went after her and fell down here. My ankle hurts bad." Tears shone in the child's eyes. "I tried to climb up the hill. I couldn't."

Hannah heard her name being called. "Jacob, we're down here. Nancy's hurt."

"I'm coming. I see her blanket."

The most wonderful thing Hannah saw was Jacob's face peering over the top of the steep incline. "She fell. I think she did something to her ankle."

Jacob descended as gracefully as she did, speed more important than caution. "I called the others. They're coming." He knelt next to them, his gaze tracking down the child's length. "Which ankle hurts?"

Nancy pointed to her left one.

Jacob tenderly took her leg into his hands and probed the area. "I don't think it's broken. Probably a sprain. We'll have to get an X-ray to be sure."

"I don't want a shot. I don't want a shot!" Nancy's voice rose to a hysterical level.

Hannah hugged her to her chest. "Honey, don't

worry about that. You need to calm down so we can get you back to the cottage."

Nancy straightened, wiping her eyes. "Where's Abby?" She scanned the surrounding terrain. "She's gone again!"

Jacob reached behind him and picked up the puppy. "She's right here, investigating a twig."

"Oh, good." Nancy sank against Hannah, grasping her as if she were a lifeline.

Hannah's gaze coupled with Jacob's. Everything would be fine now. He would take care of Nancy.

And he could take care of you.

The thought astonished Hannah. She looked away. Her feelings for Jacob were more than friendship.

"You aren't mad at me?" Nancy snuggled under her covers with her doll tucked next to her.

Hannah smoothed the girl's bangs to the side. "No. I think you realize how dangerous it can be to wander off by yourself, especially when no one knows where you are."

"I thought I could take Abby for a walk. I thought if you saw how good I can take care of her, you'd let me keep her."

"That's a decision we'll all make at the family meeting tomorrow night. There's a cat Susie would like, and Gabe wants one of Abby's brothers."

"That's great! Abby won't be alone. She'll have playmates."

"No, it isn't great. We can't have a house full of children *and* pets."

"Why not?"

"Well…" Hannah couldn't come up with a reason Nancy would understand. The little girl wouldn't accept the answer that a lot of animals running around wouldn't work. All of a sudden Hannah wasn't looking forward to the family meeting tomorrow night.

"How's your ankle?"

Nancy plucked at her coverlet. "It still hurts a little."

Hannah leaned down and kissed the child's forehead. "Thankfully it wasn't broken. You should be better in a week or so."

"Yeah, Dr. Jacob told me that. I like him."

So do I. "Good night." Hannah rose, tucked Nancy's roommate in, then quietly made her way to the door.

In the hallway she heard Jacob talking to Andy and Gabe. Earlier he'd rounded up the boys and got them ready for bed while she had taken care of the girls. As though they were a team—a family.

Hannah crossed the large living room to the picture window and stared at the darkness beyond. In the distance she saw the lights of Peter and Laura's house. Life was back to normal.

Who was she kidding?

There was nothing normal about her life at the moment. She'd discovered today she was falling in love with an enemy of her family—the man who was responsible for her brother's death.

Among all the feelings tumbling around in her

mind, guilt dominated. What would her mother say if she ever found out? Mom hadn't mentioned Jacob Hartman in years, but Hannah could just imagine what her reaction would be.

Hannah shivered as if the cold weather that had swooped down on Cimarron City in the past few hours had oozed into the cottage, into her bones.

This was one problem she'd never thought she would have. How could they overcome the history between them. They both deserved a family—but together?

A sound of footsteps behind her warned her she wasn't alone. In the pane she glimpsed Jacob approaching. She tensed. Then she caught sight of his smile and melted, all stress flowing from her.

He grasped her upper arms and pulled her back against him. "For the time being all's quiet on the home front."

The use of the word *home* in connection with Jacob sent a yearning through her she hadn't thought possible where he was concerned. He had so much to offer a woman.

But how could she be that woman?

His breath washed over her as he nibbled on the skin right below her ear, undermining all the defenses she was desperately trying to erect against him.

"After the day we had with Nancy's disappearance and our vigorous bike ride, I should be exhausted. But I'm not. I'm wide-awake."

How could this man affect her with that husky

appeal in his voice? When had her feelings for him changed? The moment she had forgiven him? Or before?

He rubbed his hands up and down her arms. "Cold?"

The humor in his question told her he knew exactly the effect he was having on her every sense. Goose bumps zipped through her, and if he hadn't been holding her up, she would have collapsed against him. "It's dropped at least twenty degrees in the last hour."

"Outside. Not in here."

He swept her around so she faced him, only inches from her. "I don't think it's going to snow."

Why was he talking about the weather when his mouth was a whisper away from hers? She balled her hands to keep from dragging his lips to hers. "If it does, it won't stick. The ground's too warm." And now she was discussing weather!

"Yes, too warm," he murmured right before settling his lips on hers.

As her arms wound about him, he pressed her close. She soared above the storm, high in the sky. Nothing was important but this man in her embrace.

When he finally drew back slightly, their ragged breaths tangled, the scent of peppermint teasing her. She would never look at a piece of that candy and not remember his kiss.

"I'd better go. It's been a long day, and I have to be at church early tomorrow." His fingers delved into her curls, his gaze penetrating into hers.

"Yes, I'm helping out in the nursery tomorrow,

so I need to get everyone moving earlier than usual."

"You want me to come to the family meeting in the evening?"

She nodded, aware of his hands still framing her face as though leaving his imprint on her. "I'm new at the family-meeting stuff so I may need your help to get it right."

"Say that again." His mouth quirked into a lop-sided grin.

She playfully punched his arm. "You heard me."

"Yes, but I like hearing you say you might need my help to get it right. I may never hear that again from your lips." The second he said the word lips his gaze zeroed in on hers.

She tingled as though his mouth still covered hers. When he lifted his regard to her eyes, a soft-ness entered his that nearly undid her. In that moment she felt so feminine and cherished.

Pulling completely away, Jacob swallowed hard. "Seriously I'll help you anytime you need it. Just ask."

"I know." Bereft without him near, she meant every word. He was a good, kind man who had made a mistake when he was young. She realized that she could forget the past now in addition to forgiving him. Peace blanketed her in an inde-scribable feeling, underscoring the rightness of what she was doing.

He backed farther away. "I can find my own way out. See you tomorrow."

She watched him stride out of the room. Turning back to the window, she glimpsed him descend the porch steps and make his way to his car.

Tomorrow she needed to go to her brother's grave and put an end to any lingering guilt. And tonight she needed to call her mother and tell her about Jacob Hartman's involvement in the refuge. She wanted to move on with her life.

Hannah made her way to her room and sat on her bed, reaching for the phone on the table nearby. Her hand quivered as she lifted the receiver and punched in her mother's number. She hadn't really talked to her in over a month. On Thanksgiving, her mother had been working and hadn't stayed on the phone for more than a minute.

"Mom, how's everything going?" Hannah asked when her mother picked up.

"Busy. Busy. You know how this time of year people seem to get sicker. My floor at the hospital has been packed this past week."

"I'm sorry to hear that." Her palms sweaty, Hannah shifted the receiver to the other ear. She didn't know how to tell her mother about Jacob. This was really something she needed to do in person. She thought about ending the conversation quickly and waiting until she could see her.

"It's late, honey. Is something wrong?"

Yes, I'm falling in love with a man you hate. "Since I didn't get to talk to you for long on Thanksgiving, I thought I would check in and see how things were going."

"Hannah, what are you not telling me? Something's wrong. I hear it in your voice."

Chewing on her lip, Hannah wiped one of her palms on her slacks. "Are you coming to see me at Christmas?"

There was a long pause, then her mother answered, "I don't know. It will depend on when I have to work. Why?"

"Because I want to see you." *Because I'm stalling.* She rubbed the other hand down her thigh. "Jacob Hartman is a doctor who lives in Cimarron City." Before she lost her nerve, she rushed on, "He's the doctor for the refuge, so I've seen him quite a bit."

"Jacob Hartman, the boy who killed Kevin?"

"Yes, Mom. I—"

"I can't believe it. I—" Her mother's voice roughened. "I—I..."

The line went dead. Hannah stared at the receiver for a few seconds, then called her mother back. She let it ring fifteen times before she finally hung up. She hadn't handled it well. She should have waited until she'd seen her mother. This news was the kind that should be given to someone face-to-face, the news that she was falling in love with the enemy.

After quizzing the groundskeeper about who was putting flowers at her brother's grave, Hannah hiked across the cemetery, enjoying the cold, crisp day. Several inches of snow had fallen overnight, but the place looked tranquil, as though the world was at peace. The quiet soothed her, especially after the night spent tossing and turning, going over and over in her head the abrupt conversation she'd had with her mother.

Near her brother's grave site, she saw a car— Jacob's new one. Since the groundskeeper had told her Dr. Hartman came once a week to change the flowers, she wasn't really surprised to see him. She stopped by a large oak and waited for him to leave.

She didn't want him to see her. The night before she had come to a decision. She needed to tell Jacob who she was, but she wanted to pick the right moment. This wasn't it. She hadn't prepared what to say to him. And because it was so important she had to consider carefully how she told him she was Kevin's younger sister, especially after messing up the phone conversation with her mother the night before.

After removing the old flowers, Jacob filled the vase with the new ones, paused for a moment, his head bowed, then pivoted away and sloshed to his car.

She waited until it had disappeared from view before she trudged to her brother's tombstone. The bright red roses, stark against the white blanket of snow, were silk. She stooped to finger the petals.

"Kevin, where do I begin?" She fortified herself with a deep gulp of the chilly air. "For so many years I was mad at Jacob Hartman for taking you away from us. I believed he had gone on with his life as though nothing had happened, living happily and unaffected by the wreck. Now I don't think that."

She reached out and traced her brother's name,

chiseled in the cold marble. The dates carved into the stone were a permanent reminder of his death at a young age. She rose.

"The groundskeeper said he comes every week. That isn't the action of a man who has moved on. Occasionally I've caught a vulnerability in him that has stunned me. He's good at hiding it, but it's there. Is it a coincidence he became a doctor? Was it because he wanted to or because that had been your dream?"

Her throat closed around her last word. The cold burrowed into her. She hugged her coat to her. "I think the Lord brought me back to Cimarron City to help Jacob. It was time to let go of my anger and forgive Jacob. I have. For the longest time I'd forgotten what kind of person you were. You would have wanted me to forgive him long ago. Better late than never." She smiled. "You know how stubborn I can be."

Hannah touched the tombstone again, comforted by her visits to Kevin's grave. Was Jacob? She hoped so because after twenty-one years she finally felt she had said her goodbyes to her brother and he didn't blame her for telling on him that last day. Kevin had never held a grudge; she had forgotten that. "I love you. I love him. I will find a way to help him heal, and I will make Mom understand. I know that's what you would want me to do."

"I like your new old car," Hannah said as she took a bite of her pepperoni pizza early Wednesday afternoon. "How come you didn't get a brand-new one? I thought you would after that piece of jun—"

"Hold it right there," Jacob interrupted her. "You're speaking about a vehicle that served me well for years."

"And years."

His chuckles vied with the lunch crowd noise in the restaurant. "Okay. I get the point. It was an old rattletrap."

"There. That wasn't too hard to admit, was it?"

He snagged her look. "Yes. I thought I was being frugal."

"Is that why you didn't buy a new one?"

"It's hard to break a habit. I've been so used to saving to pay off my loans that I just automatically do it."

"You've got to enjoy some of the fruits of your hard work. Have a little fun."

"Are you telling me I don't know how to have fun?"

"Well, no, not exactly, but what do you do for fun?"

"Bicycling?"

"That's recent."

"Let me see." He peered up at the ceiling and tapped his finger against his chin.

"Just as I suspected. You work too much and play too little."

A twinkle glinted in his dark eyes. "And what do you suggest I do about that?"

"Why, of course, play more. I think you should join us in decorating the cottage for Christmas."

"Sounds like work to me." Jacob finished the last slice of pizza.

"Decorating is fun."

"You're a woman."

"I'm glad you noticed," Hannah said with a laugh.

"It's in your genes."

"The kids wanted me to ask you."

"Oh, in that case I'll be there. What time?"

"Hold it right there. I think I'm offended. You wouldn't come when I asked, but I say something about the children and you're wanting to know what time to be there." She exaggerated a pout.

"I was going to come. I was just playing with you. Didn't you tell me I needed to play more?"

The mischief in his gaze riveted her. "I do believe you might be easy to train—I mean, teach."

His laughter filled the space between them, linking them in a shared moment. All of sudden the noise, the crowd faded from her awareness as she stared at Jacob, relaxed, almost carefree.

"Hannah, Dr. Hartman, it's good to see you two."

Reluctantly, Hannah looked away from Jacob. "It's nice seeing you, Lisa. How's the job?" Lisa had been the reason she had insisted on coming to the Pizzeria to eat before they went to see Nancy's mother.

"It's only my third day, but I like it. I saw ya from the back and wanted to say hi."

Jacob wiped his mouth with the paper napkin. "Noah told me he hired you to fill in where needed."

"Yeah, I'm learnin' all the jobs." She squared her

shoulders, standing a little taller. "There's quite a few I hafta learn, but I can do it."

"Great! I was just asking Jacob to come out on Saturday afternoon to help decorate the cottage for Christmas. If you aren't working, I'd love for you to join us, too."

"I hafta be here at five that evening."

"I can bring you back into town in time for your shift." Jacob picked up the check. "And I'll give you a ride to the farm. I can pick you up at one on Saturday."

"I'll be ready." Lisa glanced back at the counter. "I'd better get back to work."

"I know how you feel about Lisa being in Andy's life. That was so sweet of you," Hannah said around the lump in her throat.

"Believe it or not, I would love for this to work out for Lisa and Andy."

"But you still don't think it will?"

"I just don't see it through rose-colored glasses."

"And I do?"

He looked her directly in the eye. "Yes, and I'm afraid you'll be hurt when it doesn't work out."

Hannah rose. "I'm not wrong about Lisa. Did you see her at church on Sunday?"

"She was like a deer caught in headlights."

"I realize it was all new to her. But God has His ways." She could still remember when she'd pledged her heart to the Lord. The transformation, a work in progress, was life altering.

Jacob removed his wallet and laid some money

on the table. "Only time will tell." At the door he held it open for her. "C'mon, let's get this over with."

"I know Nancy's mother is a long shot, but I've got to try."

"Are you going to do this with every situation?"

She slid into the passenger seat in his car. "I will examine and evaluate every one to see if there's a way."

He gave her a skeptical look as he started the engine. "I hope you don't end up with your heart broken."

She was beginning to realize he was the only one who could do that. "Don't worry about me."

"But I do."

"That's sweet, but I'm tough."

"Yeah, right. You're like Nancy. You wear your heart on your sleeve."

She shifted, sitting up straight. "There's nothing wrong with that."

"As long as things work out."

"Like at the family meeting Sunday night?"

"Exactly." Jacob turned onto the highway that led to Deerfield. "You're blessed with the fact the kids in the cottage care about each other."

Hannah remembered the happiness on Nancy's face when the children voted for Abby to be their pet. "Like a family."

"Not any family I've been in."

The vulnerability, always below the surface, trickled into his words and pricked her heart.

Chapter Ten

Jacob pulled onto the dirt road. "I don't like the looks of this."

Hannah scanned the yard of the address she had for Nancy's mother. Trash littered the porch and literally poured out of a refrigerator without its door. Two old cars in various stages of rusting decomposition flanked the detached garage. The structure leaned to the side, threatening to crash down on the vehicle minus its engine.

"I'm glad you came with me." Hannah pushed her purse under the seat.

"Are you sure you want to do this? We can always leave." Jacob parked in front but left the engine running.

She studied the dirty windows facing them and thought she saw someone looking out. The curtain fell back in place. "No, we came this far. I need to finish this."

"No, you don't."

"Haven't you noticed how reserved and hesitant Nancy is when Andy's mother is visiting? When I try to talk to her, she won't say anything. She sucks her thumb and holds her blanket."

"As much as you'd love to fix every relationship between the children at the refuge and their parents, you won't be able to. Not every mother has maternal instincts."

"Like yours?"

"Exactly." A nerve ticked in his jaw. "I'm glad no one tried."

"You need to forgive your mother," she said, knowing firsthand how important it was to do that if you wanted to move on.

His hard gaze drilled into her, his hands gripping the steering wheel so tight his knuckles were white. "Why would I want to do that?"

"Because she's still affecting your life and will until you let go of the anger."

"I don't think I can. The things she did…"

"The Lord said in Matthew, 'For if ye forgive men their trespasses, your heavenly Father will also forgive you.'"

"I can't. I…" His voice came to a shaky halt. He drew in a breath and stared at the small house. "Someone's opening the door. Let's get this over with."

The finality in his tone ended the conversation. Hannah climbed from the car at the same time Jacob did, his expression totally void of any emotion.

But waves of underlying tension came off him as he approached the house.

A woman in her midtwenties, dressed in torn, ragged jeans and a sweatshirt pushed the screen open and stepped out onto the porch. "We don't want any. Git off my land."

A medium-sized man with a beard appeared in the entrance. Hannah's gaze fixed upon the shotgun cradled in his arms, then bounced to his face, set in a scowl that chilled her.

"Ya heard her. Git. Now." The man gestured with a nod toward the road behind Jacob and Hannah.

Jacob edged to her side and grasped her hand. "Let's do as they say."

Hannah started to move back toward the passenger door when she remembered finding Nancy crying last weekend for her mama. The sight had wrenched her heart. She halted. "Are you Abby Simons?"

The woman stiffened, still between them and the man behind her. "Who's askin'?"

A stench—a myriad of odors she couldn't even begin to identify—accosted Hannah's nostrils. "I'm Hannah Smith. I run the place that Nancy is at."

"So? What's she gone and done wrong now?" Abby planted one hand on her hip, her eyes pinpoints.

"Nothing. She's a delight to have at the house."

Abby snorted. "That's your opinion. I have nothin' to say to ya." She turned to go back inside.

"You don't want to see her?" Her stomach roiled. Hannah resisted the urge to cover her mouth and nose to block the smells coming from the house and the couple.

A curse exploded from the woman's lips. "I say good riddance. All she did was whine." She shoved past the man with the weapon.

He glared at Jacob and Hannah. "What's keepin' ya?" He adjusted the gun in the crook of his arms.

Jacob squeezed her hand and tugged her back. "We're going." He jerked open the passenger door and gently pushed Hannah into the car, then rounded the back and climbed in behind the wheel, his gaze never leaving the man holding the weapon.

Fifteen seconds later dust billowed behind his car as he raced toward the highway. He threw her a look of relief. "We could have been killed. I think they're running a meth lab."

"You do?"

"You didn't smell it?"

"I don't know how one smells."

"When we get back to Stone's Refuge, I'm calling the sheriff, although I doubt there will be any evidence left when he arrives." Jacob pressed his foot on the accelerator.

Hannah waited for him to tell her he had told her so, but he didn't. Quiet reigned as the landscape flew past them.

She'd gone into social work to help others. But perhaps Jacob was right. She was too naive. She had a lot to learn. Even if Nancy was never adopted, she was better off where she was than with her mother.

"I was wrong," Hannah finally murmured in the silence.

"About Nancy, yes. The verdict on Andy's situation is still out."

"You think there's a chance it will work?" At the moment she needed validation she wasn't totally off-the-wall about trying to reunite children with their parents, if possible.

He slanted a quick look toward her, warmth in his eyes. "His mother completed her drug-rehab program. That's a start. As well as getting a job. She's living at the halfway house for the time being, and they're wonderful support for people who are trying to get back on their feet." His gaze found hers again. "Yes, I think there's a chance."

His words made her beam from ear to ear. She felt as though she were shining like a thousand-watt bulb.

"Time will tell and don't be surprised if Lisa backslides. I remember when I quit smoking. I must have tried four or five times before I finally managed to."

"You smoked?"

"Yeah. I started when I was thirteen. I finally stopped when I was eighteen. But it was one of the hardest things I ever did. And staying off drugs will be the hardest thing Lisa does."

"Did you have help?"

He nodded. "Alice and Paul Henderson."

"I'll be there for Lisa."

"*We'll* be there for her."

Like a team. More and more she felt they were.

* * *

"I'm glad Peter suggested we cut down one of the pines on his property to use as a tree this year. Until he married Laura, I didn't do much at Christmas other than participate in some of the church functions." Jacob led one of the horses across the snow-covered meadow.

"So you don't mind doing this?" Carrying the ax, Hannah checked around her to make sure the children were keeping up with them.

"Mind? No. It's a good reason to leave work a little early this afternoon."

"This from a man who works all the time!"

"It was a little slow with the snow last night and this morning. Not too many people wanted to get out unless it was an emergency. I noticed the snow fort and snow figures out in front of the cottages. You all were busy today."

She laughed. "We had to do something with the kids home from school. I had a hard time keeping them away from the unfinished house."

"I imagine the kids are intrigued with it."

"You can say that again. I'm glad you don't mind driving in this weather. I haven't had much practice in snow."

At the edge of a grove of pines Jacob stopped and surveyed the prospective Christmas trees. "Okay, guys, which one do you want me to cut down?"

Every child with Jacob and Hannah pointed at a different one. Nancy selected a pine that was at least fifteen feet tall.

Hannah set her hands on the little girl's shoulders. "I like your vision, but that one won't fit into the living room." Then to the whole group she added, "We need a tree that is about six or seven feet tall."

"How about this?" Susie pointed to one near her.

"No, this is better." Andy went to stand by a pine off to the side.

While Terry started toward another, Hannah quickly said, "Hold it. Let's take a vote on these three. They're the only ones the right size." She waved her hand toward Susie's and two others.

Andy spun toward his. "What's wrong with mine?"

"It needs to grow a few more years." Jacob took the ax from Hannah and gave her the reins of the horse.

"Who wants Susie's?" Hannah called out, the wind beginning to pick up.

All the children raised their hands with Andy reluctantly the last one.

"Well, let's get the show on the road." Jacob approached the chosen one and began to chop it down.

The sound of the ax striking the wood echoed through the grove. The smell of snow hung in the air as clouds rolled in.

Terry bent down and scooped up a handful of the white stuff and packed it into a ball, then lobbed it toward Susie. That was the beginning of a small war held at the edge of the grove.

Hannah scurried toward Jacob to avoid being hit. "Do you want a break?"

He glanced up at the sky. "Nope. Not much time. I think it'll start snowing again soon. When that happens, I'd rather be back at the cottage sipping hot chocolate in front of the fireplace."

"We don't have one."

He paused and stared at her with a look that went straight to her heart. "Then we'll just have to use our imaginations. You do have hot chocolate?"

"Of course, with eight children in the house that's a necessity."

"We have marshmallows, too." Nancy came up to stand next to Hannah while Jacob went back to work on the seven-foot tree.

"Mmm. I love marshmallows. I guess I'd better hurry if I want a cup."

A snowball whizzed by Hannah's head. She pivoted in the direction it came. Suddenly she noticed the quiet and the reason for it. All the children were lined up a few feet from her with ammunition in their hands.

"Duck," Hannah shouted, and pulled Nancy with her behind a tree.

Jacob, in midswing, couldn't react fast enough. A barrage of snowballs pelted him from all angles. When he turned toward the crowd of kids, he was covered in white from head to toe. He shook off some of the powder, gave the ax to Hannah, then patiently walked a couple of feet toward the children with a huge grin on his face. The kids stood like frozen statues, not sure what to do.

Suddenly Jacob swooped down, made a ball and

threw it before the first child could run. Another snowball ensued then several more after it. Kids scattered in all directions. Jacob shot to his feet and raced after the nearest boy, tackling Terry. As they playfully rolled on the ground, several boys joined them and it became a free-for-all.

Hannah, with Nancy beside her, watched by their chosen tree. The sound of laughter resonated through the meadow with the girls cheering on the boys in their endeavor to overpower Jacob. Although outnumbered, the good doctor was having the time of his life if the expression of joy on his face was any clue. She knew he wanted a family. He should be a father.

And you want a family. You want to be a mother. What are you doing about that?

When a snowflake fell, followed by several more, Hannah peered up at the sky. Another hit her cheek and instantly melted. She put two fingers into her mouth and let out a loud, shrill whistle that immediately called a halt to the melee on the ground.

"In case you don't know, it's snowing again. We need to cut down our tree and get back to the cottage. Playtime is over, boys."

Amidst a few grumbles Jacob pushed to his feet, drenched from his tumble in the snow. He shoved his wet hair out of his eyes and strode to the ax Hannah held out for him.

In five minutes he yelled, "Timber," and the tree toppled to the ground. "I always wanted to do that."

Having tied the horse's reins to one of the branches of a nearby pine, Hannah moved toward it, calling to the children. "Help Dr. Jacob with our Christmas tree."

After quickly securing the pine with some rope, Jacob guided the horse toward the cottage with their tree gliding over the snow behind the animal. Snow came down faster as they reached the porch.

"I'll take the horse back to the barn," Terry said when Jacob untied the pine.

"Come right back. It'll be getting dark soon." Hannah helped Jacob drag the tree up the steps and placed it to the side of the front door. "Who's up for hot chocolate?"

Hands flew into the air.

"While I'm fixing it, change out of those wet clothes then come into the kitchen." Hannah opened the door and went into the house.

Footsteps pounded down the hallway toward the various bedrooms.

"That'll give us a few minutes of quiet." Hannah's gaze moved down Jacob's length. "I wish I had something for you to change into. Your jeans are soaking wet."

He started to remove his coat, but stopped. "I've got some sweats in my trunk. Can I use your bedroom to change in?"

Her step faltered. "Sure," she answered, trying not to imagine him in her room.

As he jogged to his car, she waved her hand in front of her face and thought about turning down the heater.

Memories of his kiss swamped her. She wanted him to kiss her again. Oh, my. She was in deep.

As she prepared the hot chocolate and a plate of cookies under the disapproving eye of Meg, the children flooded the kitchen. They snatched a mug and one cookie then fled the room, nearly knocking Jacob down in their haste.

"Whoa. What was that?" He entered as the last boy zipped past him.

"Those cookies are gonna spoil their dinner," Meg grumbled while she stirred a large pot on the stove.

"Mmm. Is that your stew?" Jacob took the last mug sitting on the counter.

Still frowning, Meg nodded.

"Then you don't have a worry. The kids love it. There won't be a drop left at the end of the meal, especially if a wonderful cook invites a certain doctor to dinner." Jacob winked at Hannah right before he took a sip of his drink.

"Not my call." The beginnings of a grin tempered Meg's unyielding expression as she swung her gaze from Jacob to Hannah.

He turned a pleading look on Hannah. "I worked up quite an appetite chopping down *your* tree."

She took a cookie off the plate. "Here. This ought to tide you over until you can eat."

His fingers grazed hers as he grasped the treat. "The important question is where will I be eating dinner?"

"Meg, we might as well make a permanent place

for Jacob at our table as often as he's been here for dinner." The image of him at one end of the table and her at the other darted through her mind. Like a family—with eight children! She should be fleeing from the kitchen as quickly as the kids did moments before. What was she doing thinking of them as a family?

"I heartily agree. Meg's cooking is much better than mine."

Meg barked a laugh. "You're cooking is nonexistent."

"Not from lack of trying."

Meg swept around with one hand on her waist and a wooden spoon in the other. "When? You work way too hard. I'm glad to see you spending more time with the children."

"I think that's our cue to leave the chef alone to create her masterpiece." Jacob grabbed the last cookie, held the door for Hannah and accompanied her from the room with Meg muttering something about him eating everything on his plate or else.

"She's a treasure. You'd better not run her off," Hannah said in mock sternness.

"I want to know what 'or else' means." He headed toward the sound of children talking in the living room.

"You're a brave soul if you dare to leave anything uneaten."

Jacob blocked her path into the room. "I enjoyed

this afternoon. Thank you for inviting me. Other than the birth of Christ, the holidays have never held much appeal to me."

"I have to admit Christmas has never been my favorite time of year." After Kevin died during December, she and her mother hadn't done much in the way of enjoying themselves during the holidays. In fact, they had ignored it until they had become Christians.

"Shh. Don't let the kids hear you say that."

"That's why we'll be going all-out this Christmas here at the house and at church."

"I'd love to help you with your activities." His gaze captured hers.

Her pulse rate spiked. "I'm glad you volunteered. Next weekend we're going to the nursing home to perform the Nativity scene. Roman can't come because of a prior commitment, but we're taking some of the animals to make the play more authentic and I could use an extra pair of hands beside Peter."

"How many animals?"

"Two lambs for the shepherds. A couple of dogs. Maybe a rabbit or two."

"I don't remember there being any dogs or rabbits in the manger."

"We thought we would dress up two of the big dogs as though they're donkeys."

Jacob tossed back his head and laughed. "I'm sure they'll love that. This production could be priceless."

"Hey, just for that, you can help with the rehearsals, too. Every night after dinner this week. We aren't nearly ready."

He wiped tears from the corner of his eyes. "Definitely priceless."

"Be careful. That box has all the ornaments in it." Hannah hurried over to help Susie carry the oversized one to the living room where Jacob and Terry were setting up the Christmas tree in its stand on Saturday afternoon.

The scent of popcorn wafted through the large cottage. Meg came out of the kitchen with two big bowls of the snack. She placed both of them on the game table. "One is for stringing. The other for eating."

A couple of the kids dived into the one for consumption, in their haste causing some of the popped kernels to fall onto the floor. Abby pounced on it.

Hannah scooped the puppy up and gave her to Nancy. "There's enough for everyone." Hannah moved the one for stringing over to the coffee table where some of the younger children sat. "Nancy, you might put Abby in the utility room until we're done."

Meg settled on the couch behind the kids working with the popcorn to assist them while Hannah opened the box with strands of twinkling white lights.

She pulled the tangled mess out and held it up, "What happened here?"

"Peter. Last year he took them down and made a

mess out of them." Meg gave Nancy who had returned without Abby a needle with a long string attached.

"Remind me not to accept his help this year with taking down the tree." Hannah sat cross-legged on the floor and searched for one end of the strand. "How many are here?"

"Four." Meg scooted over for Nancy to sit next to her while she worked on the popcorn garland.

"Maybe I should just go to town and buy new ones." Jacob squatted next to her.

"No. No, I'll figure this out. No sense in wasting money."

Fifteen minutes later Hannah finally untangled one strand completely and was on her way to freeing another.

Jacob bent down and whispered in her ear, "Ready to call uncle."

"No way. Here's one. By the time you've got it up, I should have the second string ready."

The doubtful look Jacob sent her as he rose fueled Hannah's determination, but the puppy's yelps from the utility room rubbed her nerves raw, pulling her full attention away from her task. "Nancy, please check on Abby."

Hannah had almost finished with the second strand when Abby came barreling into the room and raced toward her. The white puppy leaped into her lap, licking her face, her body wiggling so much it threw Hannah off balance.

"Nancy!" Hannah fell back with Abby on her chest now, one hand caught in the snarl of lights.

The little girl charged into the room. "Sorry. She got away from me." She pulled the puppy off Hannah.

Jacob offered her his hand, a gleam glittering in his eyes. When she clasped it, he tugged her up. "Okay?"

"Sure. Abby just gets a little enthusiastic. Laura's teenage son is going to help us with her." Hannah glanced down at the lights and groaned. The second string was twisted in with the other two.

"Uncle?"

She picked up the snarl. "Uncle."

"Let me see what I can do before ya head into town." Lisa sat next to Hannah. "I'm good at stuff like this."

Ten minutes later the lights were ready to go. Hannah purposely ignored the merriment dancing in Jacob's eyes. She corralled the remaining children who weren't working on the popcorn garlands.

"Let's get the ornaments out, so when the lights are up, we'll be ready to put them on the tree."

Three kids fought to open the box. With two fingers in her mouth, Hannah whistled, startling them. They shot up with arms straight at their sides.

She waved her hand. "Shoo. I'll unpack them and give them to y'all. Lisa, want to help me?"

Andy's mother nodded.

"There. We're done with our part." Jacob stood back from the pine and gave Terry a signal to plug the lights in.

Nancy leaped to her feet, clapping her hands. "It's beautiful."

"Yes, it is. Just wait until the ornaments are on

it. It'll be even better." Hannah peered toward Jacob who plopped into the lounge chair nearby. "And don't think your job is done. Look at this huge box of decorations."

Jacob shoved himself up. "Kids, remind me to find out what my duties are before volunteering next time."

A couple of the children giggled, setting the mood for the next two hours while everyone worked, first decorating the tree, then the rest of the house. Andy rode with Jacob to take Lisa to work. When they returned, Jacob brought large pizzas for dinner.

By the time the cottage quieted with the kids tucked into bed, exhaustion clung to Hannah, her muscles protesting her every move. "Getting ready for Christmas is tiring work." She collapsed on the couch in the living room.

"I know you may be shocked, but I have to agree with you." Jacob gestured around him at the myriad of decorations in every conceivable place. "Where did all this come from?"

"From what Laura told me, most of it was donated."

He picked up a two-foot-high flamingo with a Santa hat on its head and a wreath around its neck. "What's a flamingo have to do with Christmas?"

She shrugged. "Beats me, but it's kinda cute. Nancy sure liked it."

"She liked everything. We couldn't put it out fast enough for her."

"She's never had Christmas before. She told me her mother didn't believe in the Lord."

"Now, why doesn't that surprise me." Jacob eased down next to Hannah on the couch, grimacing as he leaned back. "After yesterday and today, I think I'll rest tomorrow."

"I think Terry said something about needing your help to build the manger Sunday afternoon."

Jacob's forehead furrowed. "And when were you going to tell me that?"

"Tomorrow when you came to help with the rehearsal."

His mouth twisted into a grim line that his sparkling eyes negated. He tried glaring at Hannah, but laughter welled up in him. He lay his head on the back cushion. "I haven't enjoyed myself like that in…" He slanted his gaze toward her. "Actually today has been great. Thank you again for including me."

The wistfulness in his voice produced an ache in her throat. "It was fun."

"It's what I think of a family doing during the holidays. The only time I had anything similar was when I lived with Paul and Alice. For three years I was part of something good." A faraway look appeared in his eyes as he averted his head and stared up at the ceiling.

Hannah dug her fingernails into her palms to keep from smoothing the lines from his forehead. She felt as though he had journeyed back in time to a past that held bad memories.

"That first Christmas with the Hendersons I was determined to stay in my room and have nothing to do with any celebration."

"Why?"

"Because in December the year before, I had killed a friend."

Chapter Eleven

Hearing Jacob say he'd killed her brother out loud tore open the healing wound. A band about Hannah's chest squeezed tight, whooshing the air from her lungs. Her mind raced back twenty-one years to the day she'd been told Kevin died in a car wreck. She heard her mother's screams then her cries all over again.

"I've shocked you, Hannah. I'm sorry. I shouldn't have said anything but…" He looked away, his jaw locked in a hard line.

His apology pulled her back to the present. She managed to shut down all memories and focus on Jacob next to her on the couch. "But what?" There was no force behind the words, and for a few seconds she wondered if he even was aware she had spoken.

When his gaze swept back to hers, the anguish in his was palpable, as if it were a physical thing she could touch. "Over the past month we've been getting closer. We've spent a lot of time together." His eyelids slid halfway closed, shielding some of his turmoil from her. "I'm not sure where this… relationship is going, but I felt you needed to know."

"What happened?" She knew one side of the story, if she could even call it that. She needed to hear his side.

"It happened twenty-one years ago, but I'll never forget that day. Ever." He reestablished eye contact with her, a bleakness in his expression now. "Kevin borrowed his parents' car one night, and we went riding. We were bored, and he wanted to practice driving. Because we were fourteen, we drove in the country so no one would catch us. After he drove for a while, he let me get behind the wheel and try my hand. Everything was going along fine until…" Jacob pressed his lips together and closed his eyes.

"Until?" Hannah covered his hand with hers, his cold fingers mirroring hers.

Sucking in a deep breath, he looked directly at her and said, "Until I lost control of the car when it hit a patch of black ice. My friend didn't put on his seat belt when we changed places, and he was thrown from the car."

Her own pain jammed her throat like a fist. It was an effort even to swallow. "What happened to you?" She'd known little about what injuries he had sustained in the wreck.

"I had a concussion, some cuts and bruises, but otherwise I was okay—physically. But after that night, nothing was the same for me. At the time I didn't believe in the Lord and had nowhere to turn." Leaning forward, he propped his elbows on his knees and buried his face in his palms.

Her heartbeat roared in her ears. She reached out to lay a quivering hand on his hunched back, stopped midway there and withdrew it. Words evaded her because she was trying to imagine dealing with something like that alone, without the Lord. He'd only been fourteen. A maelstrom of emotions must have overwhelmed him.

"How long before you went to the Hendersons to live?"

He scrubbed his hands down his face. "Too long. A year."

All the agony of that year was wrapped up in his reply. This time she touched him.

"I still have nightmares about the accident."

Her heart plummeted. All these years she had thought she and her family had been the only ones who had suffered. She'd been wrong—very wrong. "It was an *accident,* Jacob."

"Do you know one of the reasons I wanted to be a doctor? Kevin did. That's all he'd talked about."

Beneath her palm she felt him quake.

"I became a doctor. I tried to make up for my mistake, but there's always a part of me that remembers I took a life." Another tremor passed through his body. "I'll never forget Kevin's mother at the hospital. If I could have traded places with him, I would have."

Tell him who you are, Hannah thought. *No! I can't add to his pain. Not now.*

"I'm so sorry, Jacob. So sorry."

He shoved to his feet. "I'm not the one to feel sorry for. I survived."

His rising tone didn't match the despair on his face. "Yes, you survived. I thank God that at least one of you did. Your death would have deprived these children of a wonderful, caring doctor."

"You don't understand." Jacob flexed his hands at his sides. "These past few weeks with you I've been truly happy for the first time in my life. I don't deserve to be."

She rose. "Why not? How will you living a miserable life change the outcome of the wreck?"

He started to say something but snapped his mouth closed and stared off into space.

"Why are you telling me this now?"

"I thought we could date, get to know each other better, but I don't think we should now."

"Because you are happy with me?"

"Yes! These past two days getting the cottage ready for the holidays has shown me what Christmas can be like, what it would be like to have a family."

"How long do you have to suffer before it's enough?"

He plowed his hand through his hair, the tic in his jaw twitching.

"When will it be enough?"

"I don't know," Jacob shouted, then spun around

on his heel and stalked to the front door. She sank down on the couch, her whole body shaking with the storm of emotions that had swept through the room. She couldn't forget that Jacob had opened his heart to her. She had to do the same. She would pray for guidance and tell him tomorrow after church.

Hannah stood at the window, watching Jacob help Terry, Gabe and Andy build a manger for the play. The sound of laughter and hammering pounded at her resolve to find some time to be alone with Jacob and tell him who she was. He'd avoided her after church, and by the time she'd gathered all the children together, he was gone. Even when he'd come an hour ago, he'd spent little time with her, as if he'd regretted sharing something so personal with her the night before.

He lived in a self-made prison, and she was determined to free him. This was why the Lord had brought her to Cimarron City, to Stone's Refuge—to heal Jacob, a good man who had made a mistake when he was a teen.

His eyes crinkling in laughter, Jacob tousled Andy's hair. The boy giggled then launched himself at Jacob, throwing his arms around his middle. The scene brought tears to Hannah. The only time today she'd seen him relax and let down his guard was with the children.

Hannah pivoted away from the window and froze when she saw Nancy in the middle of the room, watching her with her thumb in her mouth and her doll cradled against her chest. Hannah quickly swiped away her tears. "Hi, Nancy. Have you got your costume finished for the play?"

The little girl shook her head, plucking her thumb from her mouth. "Susie said she heard you talking to Meg about visiting my mother. Susie thinks you want to get me together with her like you did Andy and his mother." Terror inched into the child's expression. "Is Mommy coming to get me?"

"No, honey."

Nancy heaved a sigh. "Good. She isn't nice like ya and Andy's mother." The little girl held up her doll. "Can we use Annie for baby Jesus?"

"Yes," Hannah murmured, relieved to see the child's terror gone from her eyes.

The child beamed. "I told Annie she could be. No one will know she's a girl."

"We'll wrap Annie in swaddling and all that will show is her face. She'll fit perfectly in the manager." Hannah gestured toward the boys in the court finishing up with the cradle.

"I'm gonna try Annie in it." Nancy raced toward the sliding-glass door that led outside.

"Hannah!"

Out of the corner of her eye she noticed Nancy carefully lay her doll into the manger. At the sound of her name being shouted again, she turned from the window as Susie came into the living room.

"I can't get this to work." The girl dropped her arms and the white sheet slid off one shoulder. "Can you help me with my costume?"

"Sure. This won't be hard to fix." Whereas she wasn't sure about her relationship with Jacob.

"Jacob, you aren't going to stay for dinner?" Hannah moved out onto the porch that evening and closed the front door behind her so the children couldn't listen.

He stopped on the top step and faced her. "It's been a long day. I have a busy week ahead of me."

He'd made sure they hadn't had a minute alone to talk. She wasn't going to let him flee, not after working up her courage to tell him everything so there were no secrets between them. "I need to talk to you."

He stiffened. "Can we another time?"

"No."

He glanced around him as though searching for a way to escape. When he directed his gaze back to her, resignation registered on his face but he remained silent.

She pointed toward the porch swing. "Let's sit down."

He strode to it and settled at one end. Hannah sank down next to him. He tensed.

"This is about what I told you last night."

The monotone inflection of his voice chilled her. She hugged her arms to her and shored up her determination. "Yes."

She tried to remember what she had planned to say, but suddenly there was nothing in her mind except a panicky feeling she was wrong, that she should remain quiet. That she would only add to his pain.

"I understand if you don't want to see me."

"Is that why you told me?" She twisted toward him so she could look into his eyes. With night quickly approaching it was becoming harder to read his expression.

"I—I'm not sure what you mean."

"It's simple. Did you tell me about your past to drive me away?"

"You have a right to know."

"Why?" A long moment of silence eroded her resolve.

She started to say he didn't have to answer her when he said, "Because I'm falling in love with you and…"

His declaration sent her heartbeat galloping. "And?"

"Isn't that enough?" He bolted to his feet and took a step forward.

She grabbed his hand and held him still. "Don't leave after telling me that."

He whirled around, shaking loose her hold. "Don't you see, Hannah? I carry a lot of baggage. That's why I don't think it's a good idea for us to become involved."

She tried to look into his eyes, but the shadows shaded them. "We all do. Please sit."

"I can't ask someone to share that."

"Why not? It's in the past. Over twenty years ago."

"I've tried to forget. I can't. I'll never be able to."

"Forget or forgive?" She stood, cutting the space between them.

"Both! My carelessness led to another's death. That may be easy for someone else to dismiss, but not me."

She desperately wanted to take him into her arms and hold him until she could erase all memories of that night twenty-one years ago—from both their memories. But the tension flowing off him was as effective as a high, foot-thick wall—insurmountable and impregnable.

"Earlier you said you're falling in love with me. That's how I feel about you."

"How—"

She placed her fingers over his mouth to still his words. "No, let me finish."

The tension continued to vibrate between them, but he nodded.

She lowered her hand and took hold of his. There was no easy way to say this to him. "I need to tell you who I am. Before I married, my maiden name was Collins. I was Kevin's little sister."

Several heartbeats hammered against her chest before Jacob reacted to her news. He yanked his hand from hers and scrambled back, shaking his head. "You can't be."

"I am. I was eight when Kevin died in the car wreck. My parents split not long after the accident and Mom and I moved away. Actually we spent many years running away."

"What kind of game are you playing?"

"I'm not playing a game."

"I killed your brother! Why are you even talking to me?"

The fierce sound of the whispered words blasted her as if he had shouted them. "I'm not going to kid you. For many years I blamed you for taking my big brother away from me. I hated you."

His harsh laugh echoed through the quiet. "And now you don't hate me." Disbelief resonated through his voice.

"No, I don't. I didn't lie when I told you I was falling in love with you."

"Please don't. I don't want to be responsible for you betraying your family on top of everything else."

"I'm not betraying them."

"I'll never be able to forget your mother yelling at me that I had destroyed her life. I dream about that."

"This isn't about my mother. This is about you and me."

"There is no you and me. I…" He took another step back until he bumped into the railing post.

She quickly covered the short distance, planting herself so he couldn't easily leave. "If that's how you feel, so be it. But I wanted you to realize how I feel."

"I know. Now I need to go." He started to push past her.

She moved into his path. "No, you don't know it all. And the least you can do for me is to listen until I'm through."

He inhaled a deep breath.

She felt the glare of his eyes boring into her although darkness now cloaked the porch totally.

"When I came back to Cimarron City, I discovered you were still living here and a doctor. At first I didn't realize you were the pediatrician for Stone's Refuge, but when I discovered that, I considered leaving. I didn't see how I could work with the man who killed my brother."

"It does seem unbelievable." Sarcasm inched into his voice as he tried to distance himself as much as she allowed.

"Have you forgotten what Christ has taught us? To forgive those who trespass against us?"

"Yeah, but—"

"But, nothing." She gripped his arms. "I have forgiven you for what happened to Kevin. It was an *accident.*"

His muscles beneath her palms bunched.

"You're a good man who deserves to really live his life. You've paid dearly over the years for the wreck. Don't you think it's time you stop beating yourself up over it?"

"Because you say so?"

She thrust her face close to his. "Yes!"

For a long moment tension continued to pour off him, then as if he had shut down his emotions, he closed himself off. "Is that all?"

All! She nodded, her heart climbing up into her throat.

"May I leave now?"

"Yes." She backed away from him.

It didn't matter to him that she had forgiven him. He couldn't forgive himself.

The sound of his footfalls crossing the porch bombarded her. This was the end.

She couldn't let him walk away without trying one more time to make him understand. "Jacob."

He kept walking toward his vehicle.

"Jacob, stop!"

He halted, his hand about to open the car door. The stiff barrier of his stance proclaimed it was useless for her to say anything. He wouldn't really hear.

She had to try anyway.

Hannah hurried toward him, praying he didn't change his mind and leave. She positioned herself next to him, hoping he would look at her.

He stared over the roof of the car into the distance. The lamplight that illuminated the sidewalk to the house cast a golden glow over them. She could make out the firm set to his jaw and the hard line of his mouth slashing downward.

"When I realized I'd finally forgiven you for what had happened to Kevin, I was free for the first time in twenty-one years. That's what forgiveness can do for you. Let it go."

He cocked his head to the side. "And just when did you decide to forgive me?"

"It wasn't a sudden revelation. But I knew when you took care of me and the children during the strep outbreak."

"And all the time before that?"

"I was fighting my growing feelings for you."

"And you lost."

"I don't look at it as losing. I want to see where our relationship can lead."

"Nowhere, Hannah. Nowhere. So why waste our time?" He wrenched open the door and climbed inside his car.

A few seconds later the engine roared to life, and Jacob sped away. As the taillights disappeared from view, she vowed she wouldn't give up on him.

Hannah leaned against the wall in the back of the rec room at the nursing home as the children began their play about the birth of Jesus. She scanned the crowd one more time, hoping she had overlooked Jacob, but he was nowhere in the audience. Her gaze fell upon Lisa in the front row with Cathy and she was glad that at least Andy had his mother at the play. But no Jacob, although he had promised the kids he would be at their production, via a phone call to Terry. Jacob hadn't been at the house in a week. He was avoiding her. She didn't need it written in the sky to know what Jacob was doing. She'd even thought briefly—very briefly—that maybe one of the children would get sick and she would have to take them to see Dr. Jacob.

Not having dated much, she wasn't sure what to do now. She missed him terribly. She hadn't realized how much until day three and she had reached for the phone at least ten times to call him. She hadn't, but the desire to had been so strong she had shaken with it.

Laura slid into place next to her and whispered,

"He'll be here. He doesn't break a promise to the kids."

"There's always a first time." Hannah checked her watch for the hundredth time. "He has one minute before Susie and Terry appear as Mary and Joseph."

No sooner had she said Joseph than Jacob slipped into the room and eased into a chair in the back row at the other end of the room from where she was. Hannah straightened, folding her arms across her body.

Laura turned her head slightly toward her and cupped her hand over her mouth. "I told you he would be here."

"Shh. The play is about to start. I don't want to miss a word of it."

"Who are you kidding? You've heard the lines until I'm sure you can recite every one of them."

Hannah really tried to follow the children as they reenacted the story of the birth of Christ, but she continually found herself drawn back to Jacob, his strong profile a lure she couldn't resist. She came out of her trance when one of the lambs escaped and charged down the aisle toward the door by Jacob, baaing the whole way. The play stopped, and everyone twisted around in his seat to follow the animal's flight. Dressed in a gray suit, Jacob sprang to his feet and blocked its path to freedom, tackling it to the floor, its loud bleating echoing through the room.

"Got her." Jacob struggled to stand with the squirming animal fighting the cage of his arms.

As though the first lamb had signaled a mass bolt for all the animals, the other one broke free, probably because the young boy holding him had let go. Then the two dogs, portraying donkeys, up until this point perfectly content to sit by their handlers, chased after the second sheep. Kids scattered in pursuit of their fleeing pets.

Shocked at how quickly everything had fallen apart, Hannah watched the pandemonium unfold, rooted to her spot in the back along the wall. Then out of the corner of her eye, she saw a dog dart past her. She dived toward the mixed breed and captured it. Thankfully the mutt was more cooperative than Jacob's lamb. Taking the large dog by his collar, she led it back to the front where Peter was trying to bring some kind of order to the chaos.

Sprinkles of laughter erupted from the audience until all the elders joined in. One woman with fuzzy gray hair in the front row laughed so hard tears were running down her rouged cheeks, streaking her makeup.

"I think the show is over," Hannah said, clipping a leash on the dog she had.

"At least they were near the end." Jacob put his lamb down but held the rope tightly. "I'm not tackling this one again."

Hannah gave Jacob the leash then held up her hands to try and quiet the audience while Peter, Laura and Meg gathered the rest of the animals and the kids. Several times she attempted to say, "If everyone will quiet down," but that was as far as she got because no one was listening.

"Remember laughter is the best medicine." Jacob struggled to keep the lamb next to him.

Five minutes later only after Hannah whistled, the last strains of laughter died but whispering among the residents and children began to build. She quickly said, "There are refreshments in the lobby. The children made them."

The word *refreshments* sparked the interest of several elders in the front, and they started moving toward the exit.

Slowly the rec room emptied with Laura and Meg taking the children who were serving the food.

Peter took one of the lambs and headed for the door. "I'll be back for the others."

That left Hannah and Jacob trying not to look at each other. Unsuccessful, she finally stepped into his line of vision. "We should talk."

He swung his gaze to her. "I'm not ready. I don't know if I'll ever be ready now that I know who you are."

"You make it sound like I've changed somehow. That I'm a different person. I'm still Hannah Smith. That's my legal name now. Not Hannah Collins."

"And every time I look at you I see Kevin. I should have seen the resemblance. You have the same hair and eyes."

"Like millions of others."

He started to say something when Peter reentered the room. "I can help you with your animals."

Jacob lifted the lamb into his arms, then tugging on the dog leash, walked toward his friend.

"Me, too." Hannah led her mutt along behind Jacob.

"I'll get the props," Peter called out.

Hannah barely heard the man, she was so intent on catching up with Jacob. She reached him in the parking lot at Peter's truck. He hoisted the lamb into its crate, then the dog. After taking care of the animals, Jacob stepped around Hannah and started to make his way back inside. She stopped him with a hand on his arm.

"Jacob—"

"Why did you tell me you were Kevin's sister?" His question cut her off.

And knocked the breath from her. The streetlight accentuated the harsh planes of his face, but distress rang in his voice. "Because I didn't want any secrets between us. You had shared yours. I had to."

"I feel like I'm reliving that night all over again."

She squeezed his arm as though to impart her support. "I didn't tell you to put you through that."

"What did you think I was going to do?"

"I don't know. But it was the right thing to do."

"For you."

She peered toward the building and saw Peter emerge. Through the floor-to-ceiling windows Hannah glimpsed the children playing host to the residents, serving them the refreshments and talking with them.

"The kids missed you this week. They've gotten used to you coming to see them a lot. Please don't stay away because of me."

Jacob shifted away from her. "I've been especially busy. It's flu season."

"They wanted me to ask you to Sunday dinner tomorrow."

Jacob closed his eyes for a few seconds. "I can't." He strode away, not toward the nursing home but toward his car.

Her legs weak, Hannah leaned back against Peter's truck as the man came up with a box full of props.

"What's wrong with Jacob?" Peter slid the items into the bed of his pickup.

"I think I've ruined everything."

Chapter Twelve

"Dr. Jacob, you came!" Andy launched himself at Jacob and hugged him. "We've missed you."

"Where's Hannah? How's she feeling?" Jacob walked into the cottage, the scent of a roast spicing the air. His stomach rumbled its hunger.

"She's in her office," Susie said, looking too cheerful for someone who was concerned about Hannah's health.

"Office?" The way the twelve-year-old had described it on the phone to him half an hour ago, Hannah was dragging herself around the house, refusing to go to a doctor but desperately needing to see one. Reluctantly, he had agreed to come see what he could do.

Susie shrugged. "You know Hannah. She doesn't stop working for anything."

Knowing the way, Jacob headed back to Hannah's office. Before rapping on the door, he peered back at the end of the hallway and met several pairs of eyes watching him. The kids ducked back around the corner.

He knocked and waited for Hannah to invite him in. When half a minute passed and there wasn't a reply, he tapped his knuckles against the wood harder. Concerned, he decided to give her a couple more seconds before he went in without an invitation.

"Come in," a sleepy voice murmured from inside the room.

He inched the door open and peeped around it to find Hannah with her legs propped up in the lounger and only one dim lamp to illuminate the office. She blinked several times, as though disorientated, and straightened the chair to its upright position.

"Jacob, why are you here?" Drowsiness coated each word.

He slipped inside, aware of the children's whispering voices down the hall.

"Susie called and told me you weren't feeling well and wouldn't go see a doctor. She sounded very concerned, so I reassured her you would be all right. She wouldn't believe me until I agreed to come check you out." He crossed the room, pulling behind him a lattice-back chair to sit in. "What's wrong?"

She scrunched up her forehead, then rubbed her fingers across it. "Just a headache. Nothing serious and Susie knew that. I took some pills and came in here to close my eyes until they started working. I must have fallen asleep."

"Then you're okay? No fatal disease?"

She chuckled. "Not that I know of."

"I think Susie should take up acting lessons. She had me convinced you were at death's door."

"I appreciate the concern, but I'm fine. Well, except the headache isn't totally gone. Nothing I can't handle, though." She sent him a smile that went straight to his heart and pierced through the armor he had around it.

"Then if you're all right, I'll be heading home." He started to stand.

"What time is it?"

Weary from many sleepless nights and long days at work, he sank back down and looked at his watch. "Six."

"Stay for dinner. I think what's really behind this little incident is that the kids miss you and want to see you more." Her gaze bored into him. "And so do I."

"To tell you the truth I've missed...coming here." He'd missed seeing the children but most of all Hannah. Yet how could he be with her, knowing who she really was? This woman had haunted his dreams lately. It was hard to look at her and not remember Kevin.

"I'm not going away. You need to learn to deal with my presence. Don't let the children suffer because of the past. When I first came to Stone's Refuge, I had to do the same thing. And I did."

He released a slow breath. "You play hardball."

She scooted to the edge of the lounger. "On occasion. When it's important."

"And this is important?"

"Yes."

He agreed—not just because of the children but because of the woman whose smile played havoc with his heart. Although there was no way he could now see a future with Hannah, maybe he could find a compromise and be her friend, especially if there were always kids around them.

He rose at the same time she did and nearly collided with her. Backing away quickly, he offered her a grin, hoping he appeared nonchalant when he didn't feel in the least that way. "Then I'll stay for dinner."

"No doubt Andy will want you to read him a bedtime story. He has a lot to tell you about him and his mother. She comes out here when she's not working and helps around the cottage."

"Noah's told me she's doing a good job at the restaurant."

"She's hoping to move out of the halfway house soon."

"What's the next step for her and Andy?" Jacob strode to the door but didn't open it yet.

"Once Lisa gets her own place, Andy will stay with her overnight, and we'll see how that goes."

"I hope for his sake that you're right about Lisa, but be careful. It doesn't take much for a drug addict to backslide." He hurriedly pushed away the memories of his own mother's downward spiral. Hopefully Lisa and his mother were different.

"Mom, let me help you with your bags." Masking her surprise behind a smile, Hannah opened the front door wider and scooped up one of the pieces of luggage. "Why didn't you tell me you were coming?" *Why didn't you return my calls?* was the question she really wanted to ask but not in the foyer where someone could overhear their conversation.

"I wasn't sure until a few days ago, and then I just decided to surprise you."

"How long are you staying?"

Karen Collins chuckled. "You know me. I never travel lightly. The weather in Oklahoma can be so unpredictable. It could snow one day and be warm and sunny the next." Her mother came into the cottage. "Hon, once when I lived here I can remember the weather dropping forty degrees in half a day. So where do I stay?"

"In my bedroom. I'll show you, then I'll introduce you to the kids. They're in the kitchen helping Meg with the Christmas cookies for the birthday party for Jesus tonight at the church."

"All eight of them?"

"Yes, it's a big kitchen." Hannah walked down the hall to her bedroom door and pushed it open to allow her mother to go inside first.

"And this is a nice-sized room, too."

"My bathroom is through there." Hannah pointed

toward the entrance on the other side of the large bed. "I also have an office off the kitchen."

"And you like living here with eight children?"

"I love it." For the first time in years Hannah felt as if she had put down roots. To her the cottage was her home.

Her mother lifted her bag onto the king-size bed and opened it. "Where do I put my things?" When Hannah glanced from one piece of luggage to the other, Karen hurriedly added, "I'll only unpack part of my clothes."

"Well, in that case I have enough space in my closet, and I can clear out a drawer for you in the dresser."

"I know how much you've wanted kids in your life. Any prospects of a husband?" Hannah's mom hung up a dress and started back toward the bed.

As though they hadn't talked about Jacob at all, her mother as usual was avoiding the real issue and probably why she was here in the first place. "Yes, there is a man I'm interested in." Dread encased Hannah in a cold sweat.

Karen peered up at her as she shook out a shirt. "You are? That's wonderful. Who?"

The air in Hannah's lungs seemed to evaporate with that last question. She'd tried to tell her mother over the phone, but her mom had ignored all of her follow-up calls after the disastrous conversation. "Jacob Hartman."

Karen dropped the shirt. "I thought he was just the doctor here. Nothing more."

"Mom, I know this is a shock, but you wouldn't talk to me." Hannah rushed forward and drew her mother to the sitting area across the room. "Please don't say anything until you hear me out."

Karen pressed her lips together, surprise still registering on her face.

"I didn't realize Jacob was involved with Stone's Refuge until after I accepted the job here. I couldn't walk away. This is the perfect job for me." Hannah's heartbeat pounded like a kettledrum in a solemn procession. "Jacob is wonderful with the children. He's kind, caring and is trying desperately to make up for what happened all those years ago."

"You've forgiven him for what he did to your brother?"

The drumming beat of Hannah's heart increased. "It's the Christian thing to do, Mom. I know how you feel, but please give him a chance."

Karen shook her head slowly. "I don't know if I can. I never imagined you were dating the man." Again she shook her head. "Working with him is one thing, but getting involved romantically…"

"Get to know him like I did, and you'll see what a good man he is."

"Until you called a few weeks ago, I hadn't thought about him in a long time. He consumed so much of my life for years that once I gave myself to Christ I just pushed memories of him away. I know how the Lord feels about forgiveness, but…" Tears shone in her mother's eyes. "It's so hard. Kevin is dead because of him."

"It was an accident, Mom."

"But he walked away from the wreck with few injuries."

"He may not have been injured much physically, but he was emotionally. His scars run deep."

"Will he be here tonight?"

"Yes."

"When is he coming?"

With a glance at her watch, Hannah rose. "He should be here within the hour. He promised the kids he would bring pizza tonight when he goes to pick up Andy's mother at the restaurant. She's going with us to church later."

"Is that the woman you've been helping?"

"Yes. I need to get back to the kitchen to help with the cookies." Hannah put her hand on the door. "Are you coming?"

Her mother pushed to her feet. "I'm really tired, honey. I'm going to rest for a while. You go on without me and don't worry about me."

Out in the corridor Hannah stared at the closed bedroom door, her stomach in snarls. She was all her mother had in the way of family, and she was afraid her mom wouldn't come out whenever Jacob was at the cottage.

Lord, please help Mom forgive Jacob as You helped me. I love both of them.

Hannah opened the back door to admit Jacob, who brought their dinner. "The kids were wondering where you were."

"Just the kids?" He waded his way through the mob of children, all wanting one of the pizza boxes.

"Me, too. I'm starved." She took several containers from him and began opening them. "Everyone, act civil. There's plenty to go around."

Jacob stepped away as soon as he lifted the lids and brushed some snowflakes from his coat and hair. "What have you all been doing? They've worked up quite an appetite."

"Is it snowing bad?" Hannah glanced at the window, but the curtains were drawn.

"No, not too much." Jacob removed his overcoat and slung it over the back of a chair.

While all the children were filling their plates with pizza, Andy stood off to the side, his gaze glued to the back door. "Where's Mom?"

Jacob looked around. "She isn't here?"

"No." Alarm pricked Hannah. "She was supposed to ride out here with you."

"The guy behind the counter said she left earlier. I thought she hitched a ride here with someone else." Jacob headed for the wall phone and punched in some numbers.

Concern creased Andy's forehead. "Where is she?"

"She's probably running late. Go on and get something to eat before there's nothing left." Hannah hoped she concealed her rising fear that all wasn't right with Lisa. She didn't want Andy to worry needlessly.

Coming up next to Jacob, she heard him say, "Give us a call if she arrives there."

When he hung up, she motioned with a nod for them to go into the hallway where Andy wouldn't overhear what they said. "Did you call the halfway house?"

"Yes, and they haven't seen her since she left for work this morning."

"What should we do?"

"Nothing."

"Nothing? We need to do something."

Jacob frowned. "What do you suggest?"

"I don't know. Go look for her."

"Where?"

Hannah shrugged, helplessness seizing her.

Andy poked his head around the kitchen door. "Something's wrong with Mom, isn't it?"

Hannah knelt in front of the boy and clasped his arms. "We don't know, hon."

Tears crowded his eyes. "Please find her."

Hannah glanced over her shoulder at Jacob, who nodded once. "Do you know anywhere she liked to go? A favorite place?"

Sniffling, Andy studied the floor by his feet. Finally he shook his head. "When she was gone, I never knew where she went."

Hannah rose. "I think Jacob and I have time to go to the halfway house and check with them before we go to church."

Andy's eyes brightened. "Maybe she went back to the old neighborhood."

"We'll go there, too." Jacob came forward. "Now, will you do me a favor, Andy?"

"Yes."

"Go eat some dinner and make sure everyone is ready to go to church on time."

"Sure." Andy straightened his slumped shoulders.

After the boy disappeared into the kitchen, Hannah asked, "Do you think she went back to her boyfriend?"

"Possibly. We've got a couple of hours to find her. Let's go."

"Will you tell Meg where we're going and if we aren't back in time to get Peter and Laura to take the children to church? I'll need to get my purse. Meet you back here in a few minutes."

Without waiting for an answer, Hannah hurried toward her bedroom. This wasn't the time for her mother to come out in case she had changed her mind. She needed to tell Jacob about her mom's surprise visit. In the quiet of his car would be the best place.

In her bedroom, she put a blanket over her mother who slept on top of her coverlet, then grabbed her purse and quickly left. Two minutes later she sat next to Jacob as he pulled away from the cottage.

"Everything okay in the kitchen?" Hannah fidgeted with the leather handle of her purse.

"Yeah. There's not much pizza left. I should have bought another one. You won't have anything to eat when we get back."

She pressed her hand over her constricted

stomach. "I couldn't eat even if pizza was my favorite food."

"It isn't?" Mock outrage sounded in his voice. "Don't tell Noah."

"It'll be our secret." She paused. "Speaking of secrets. Well, this isn't exactly a secret. More of a surprise."

He slid a look toward her as he turned onto the highway. "What?"

"My mother came to visit this afternoon for a few days. She wanted to spend Christmas with me, and her employer gave her the time off at the last minute."

His harsh intake of air was followed by silence.

"This is just like Mom. When the mood strikes, she gets up and goes somewhere. She doesn't like staying still for long in any one place. There were many times while I was growing up that I left my things in boxes rather than unpack. It was easier that way." She heard her nervous chattering and wished she could see Jacob's face but the dark hid it.

"Does she know about me being involved in Stone's Refuge?"

"Yes."

"Before or after she came."

"Before."

"I'm sure that made her day. Why is she really here?"

"That's a good question. One I don't have an answer to."

Silence ate into her composure. She rubbed her

thumb into her palm and tried to think of a way to make everything all right. *Lord, what do I do? How do I fix this?*

"Hannah, I'm sorry you had to tell your mother. I imagine that wasn't a nice reunion for you two."

"I told my mother that I had forgiven you for what happened with Kevin, that I cared about you." *That I want to be more than friends with you,* she wanted to add but realized at the moment Jacob wouldn't want to hear that.

His derisive laugh taunted her words. "She was thrilled, no doubt."

"I love my mother, but we don't always see eye to eye on things. This will just be another item added to the bottom of a long list."

"Don't you mean, added to the top?"

Before she could answer him, her cell phone blared with a drumroll. She fumbled for it in her purse and flipped it open. "Hello."

"Hannah?" A voice, barely audible, came through.

"Yes, who is this?"

"I'm in trouble."

Hannah sat up straight. "Lisa, where are you?"

"I'm near my old apartment. He's so angry."

"Who?"

"My ex-boyfriend," Lisa said in a raspy whisper.

"Jacob and I are on our way. We'll be—" The connection went dead.

Hannah snapped her cell closed. "Please hurry. Lisa's near her boyfriend's apartment. Something's wrong. She sounds…" She searched for a word to describe what she heard in the woman's voice beside fear.

"High?"

"Likely."

Jacob pressed down on the accelerator. He remembered the times he found his mother stoned. The memories, one after another, left him chilled in the car's heated air. That last night before the state took him away from her, the paramedics had said she'd been a few minutes away from death. If he hadn't come home… He shuddered and increased his speed even more.

Chapter Thirteen

"Oh, great! It's snowing even harder now. Normally I love to see it on Christmas Eve. Not this year." Hannah gripped the door handle, prepared to jump from the car the second Jacob parked.

"Why did she go with her ex?"

"Some women have a hard time breaking ties with men who've been in their life, even ones who have abused them."

Jacob took a corner too fast, and the car fishtailed on a slick area. The color leached from his face as he struggled to control his vehicle.

She gasped. For a few seconds her brother's wreck flittered across Hannah's mind as a telephone pole loomed ahead.

Steering into the skid, he slowed his speed. Finally he managed to right the car, missing the curb and pole by a couple of feet. "Sorry," he bit out between clenched teeth, his white-knuckle grasp on the wheel tightening.

"It's okay. We need to get to Lisa before her boyfriend finds her."

"It's not okay!" Although the words came out in a harsh whisper, the power behind them hung in the air, reinforcing the barrier that he had erected between them. "I could have…"

His unfinished sentence lingered. She touched his arm.

He swallowed hard. "I know better. I couldn't live with myself if I caused something to happen to you, too." He retreated into stony silence as he negotiated the city streets.

"I forgave you, Jacob. There were no strings attached to that forgiveness."

"How could you?"

She felt as though she was fighting for the most important thing in her life. "Because I love you. Love yourself."

He shook off her arm, his jaw set in a grim line. His scowl told of the war of emotions raging inside him. She wanted so much to comfort him but knew he would reject it—reject her. All she could do now was pray and turn it over to the Lord.

When the apartment building came into view, Hannah bent forward, scouring the area around it for any sign of Lisa. Jacob brought the car to a stop in front. Hannah leaped from the vehicle and raced toward the entrance.

Jacob halted her progress. "What do you think

you're doing?" His hand immediately fell away as if touching her was distasteful.

Snowflakes caught on her eyelashes. She blinked and looked up into his fierce expression. "Going inside to see if Lisa is with him."

"Let's check outside first. That's where she was when she called."

"Okay, I'll look down this side. You go over there." She waved toward the area across the street.

"No, we go together in case the boyfriend is looking for her, too."

"But it will go faster if—"

"I don't want you meeting up with him alone." His determination, a tangible force, brooked no argument.

"Fine. Then let's get moving. We're wasting time." Frustrated, worried, she stalked down the street.

Passing an alley, Hannah walked down its length, inspecting every place someone could hide. Nothing. Back out on the sidewalk, she continued, stopping at the quick market on the corner, the only place open on Christmas Eve.

"Let's check inside. Maybe she's hiding in here since it's cold and snowing," she said as she entered the store.

While she went up and down the aisles, Jacob questioned the clerk at the counter. When she finished her search, she came back to his side.

"If she comes back in, tell her Jacob and Hannah are looking for her and to wait here." Jacob took her elbow and led the way to the door. "She was here about fifteen minutes ago, using the phone in the back. When a man came in that fits the description of her boyfriend, she must have fled. The clerk didn't see her leave, but he thinks she went out the back way."

"Then he may not have found her."

"The clerk told the man she was on the phone in the back."

"No! How could he?"

"He was scared. He knows who Carl is and doesn't want to have any trouble with him."

"Did he call the police?"

"No."

Lord, please put Your protective shield around Lisa.

"We've got to find her first." Hannah rounded the corner of the store, making her way to the back where Lisa would have come out.

Footsteps in the continually falling snow led away from the door, heading toward an alley nearby. Another set had joined the first.

"She's running." Jacob pointed at the long stride between each print.

"He isn't, as if he's stalking her and knows he'll catch her."

"With this snow, it'll be hard for her to hide from him."

"But we can track her, too." Hannah hurried her pace.

The darkness of the alley obscured part of the footprints, but the occasional light from a window showed them the way—as well as Carl. At one place Lisa must have tried to go into a building, but the door was locked.

Jacob slowed, putting his arm out to halt Hannah. "Call 9-1-1."

She squinted into the dimness and glimpsed what he'd seen. A still body curled into a ball in the snow, a fine layer of the white stuff covering the person. She dug into her pocket and pulled out her cell, making the call while Jacob stooped and brushed the snow off the body, revealing Lisa.

After talking to the 9-1-1 operator, Hannah knelt next to Jacob. "Is she alive?"

"Yes." Removing a penlight from his pocket, he began to check out Lisa's injuries. "She's got a lump on the back of her head."

A snow-covered pipe lay a few feet away, a stream of light from the building illuminating it.

A moan escaped Lisa's lips. "No, don't." She raised her arm as though she were fending off a blow. Her eyes bolted open. She saw Jacob, and her arm fell to the pavement. "I'm sorry. I'm sorry." Tears streamed down her cheeks and blended with the melted snow on her face.

Hannah leaned close. "Lisa, I'm going to wait for the police and ambulance at the end of the alley. You're going to be all right. Jacob will take care of you."

Jacob paced the waiting room, wearing a path in front of Hannah's chair. "We should have heard something by now."

"Carl beat her up pretty badly. Thankfully Lisa was conscious enough to tell us what drug she took before she passed out again."

Jacob paused before her. "Let's hope the police have brought him in by now."

"One less drug dealer on the streets."

"But for how long?"

"Do you think Lisa will testify against him?"

"No." He pivoted and started pacing again. "She's afraid of him and rightly so."

"We've got to be there for her. Maybe then she will."

"Maybe." But skepticism drenched his voice.

An emergency-room doctor appeared in the doorway. "Jacob, I heard you found the woman. Does she have any kin?"

"A son staying at Stone's Refuge. Otherwise, I don't think so. How is she?"

"A concussion, two cracked ribs and some cuts and bruises. I think the man had a ring on that left his mark as he was pounding on her."

Chilled, Hannah stood and clasped her arms, running her hands up and down to warm herself. "May we see her now?"

"They're taking her upstairs to a room. Give them fifteen minutes to get her settled in, then you can see her. I want to keep her overnight for observation. If she does okay, she can go home tomorrow."

After the doctor left, Hannah sighed. "We need to get Andy. I promised him we would."

Jacob glanced at his watch. "He should be at the church with the others right now. I'll go pick him up and bring him back to see his mother while you go talk to her."

"She'll want to see you and thank you, Jacob."

"I don't know if that would be a good idea."

"Because she had a relapse?"

"Some things never change."

"Lisa is human. She made a mistake. We all do. God forgives us thankfully, so the least we can do is try to do the same."

His gaze sliced through Hannah. "I'll be back later with Andy." Jacob strode from the waiting room before he said something he would regret. He'd heard the censure in her voice. But Hannah hadn't lived with a drug addict. He had. His mother had ruined her life and had been well on the way to doing the same with his.

No, you did a good job of that yourself that night you killed Kevin. What she started, you finished.

His guilt that was always there swelled to the foreground, threatening to swamp him. Up until the appearance of Hannah in his life he'd managed to cope with what he had done. Now he didn't know if he could continue to work with the children at Stone's Refuge and see her. He'd thought he could, but he wanted more. He wanted a wife and a family—with Hannah. But how could they ever be really happy with what happened always hanging between them? How could she have really forgiven him?

Jacob found a parking space in the nearly full lot

at the church and walked toward the entrance. The snow had stopped and a white blanket muffled the sounds, making it serenely quiet. Christmas music wafted from the sanctuary, reminding him how special this time of year was. He entered the place of worship and stood in the back, searching for the large group from the refuge. He caught Peter's gaze, and his friend leaned around Laura to let Meg know Jacob was there.

Andy exited the pew and started for him. Following close behind the boy was a woman whose image was burned into his memory. For a few seconds the remembrance whisked him back to the hospital corridor where Hannah's mother had accused him of ruining her life, that he might as well have killed her, too. Emotions so strong he staggered back a couple of steps inundated him as his gaze locked with Kevin's mother's.

Around him the congregation sang "O Holy Night" while Jacob desperately tried to compose himself enough to deal with her and Andy. He knew one thing as the distance disappeared between—that he didn't want the parishioners to witness the scene. Fumbling for the handle, he wrenched open the door to the sanctuary and escaped out into the empty lobby.

Why now, Lord?

No answer came as Andy and Karen Collins halted in front of him. His attention remained glued to the older woman, who was slightly heavier and with strands of gray hair, but otherwise the same as twenty-one years before.

"Dr. Jacob, is my mother all right? Did you find her?"

Andy's voice drew his gaze to the boy standing half a foot away, his head upturned, his eyes large with fear and worry in their depths.

Jacob forced a smile of reassurance. "She's going to be fine."

"Where is she?"

"At the hospital."

Panic widened the boy's eyes even more. "She's hurt!"

"Hannah is there with her. I've come to take you to see her." Jacob settled his hands on the boy's shoulders, compelling the child's full attention. "She has a lump on her head and some cuts and bruises, but she'll mend just fine. She's going to need you to be strong. Can you do that for her?"

Andy drew himself up tall. "Yes."

"Where's your coat?"

The boy pointed toward the hallway that led to the classrooms. "Back there."

"Go get it, then we'll leave."

The second the child disappeared down the corridor Jacob's gaze fastened on Kevin's mother. So many things he wanted to say swirled in his mind, but none formed a coherent sentence.

"Hannah said you were wonderful with the children. She's right."

Her words, spoken with no anger, confounded Jacob. He stared at her, speechless.

"When Hannah first told me today you two were

more than associates, that you were…friends, I didn't know what to say to her. After she left to go with you, I had a long talk with God. I wanted to tell you that I've forgiven you for what happened, too. As my daughter pointed out to me, it was an accident that ended tragically for my son. What I said to you in the hospital that day was grief talking, but it took me years to realize that. It took finding the Lord and my daughter's example to see what I needed to do. I'm sorry for what I said."

Jacob heard her, but the words wouldn't register. "How can you say that?"

She smiled. "Stop blaming yourself for something that was out of your control."

Out of the corner of his eye, Jacob glimpsed Andy coming back. He rushed to the boy and clasped his hand. "We need to get to the hospital," was all he could think to say.

A few minutes later he headed his car away from the church, still grappling with what Hannah's mother had said.

"You aren't kidding me, are you? Mom is okay?"

"I promise. I'd never kid you about something like that. She's staying overnight at the hospital and hopefully will go home tomorrow."

"I won't get to see her on Christmas?"

"I'll make sure you do. I'll pick her up and bring her to the cottage to spend some time with you if the doctor says it's okay."

Andy heaved a long sigh. "Good. I don't want her being alone on Christmas. She needs me."

Shouldn't it be the other way around? "You aren't mad at her for all that's happened?" The question slipped out before Jacob could snatch it back.

"No."

"Why not?"

"I love her."

Is love the key? If you love someone enough, you forgive them?

God loved us so much that he gave His only son for our salvation. Hannah had said Christ has taught us to forgive, that she had learned from the Master Himself.

Could he? Can the Lord forgive him for taking another's life? Could he forgive himself for surviving the car wreck? Could he forgive his mother for his childhood?

If he wanted any kind of life, he needed to figure that out.

"Where's Dr. Jacob?" Hannah asked as Andy came into the hospital room.

"He needed to go see someone. He told me Peter will come and take us home." The boy walked to his mother's bed and took her hand.

Lisa's eyes fluttered open. "Andy," she said groggily.

"How are you?" The child's voice thickened with tears.

"Hey, baby. Don't cry. I'm gonna be fine thanks to Hannah and Jacob." She closed her eyes for a few seconds. "I love ya."

Andy lay his head near his mother's. "I love ya, Mom. Dr. Jacob said ya could come to the cottage tomorrow if the doctor says so."

"That's…great. I can't…" Sleep stole Lisa's next words.

"Let's go home and let your mother rest. You'll see her tomorrow morning. We'll come up here early."

"Are ya sure?"

"Yep. It won't really be Christmas without your mother there." Hannah draped her arm over Andy's shoulder and led the way into the hallway.

At the elevator the doors swished opened, and Peter stepped off.

"We were coming downstairs to wait for you." Hannah let the elevator close behind her employer. "Church is over already?"

"No, but I thought I would come right away. It's been a long day for you all."

"Yes, and it's not over yet." She needed to find Jacob.

"My car is in the front parking lot." Peter punched the down button.

"Peter, can you do me a favor?" Hannah got on the elevator when it arrived.

"Sure."

"I need to pay a visit to someone. Can you drop me off then take Andy to the cottage?"

"Yes."

Andy glanced back at Hannah. "Hey, are ya gonna visit the same person as Dr. Jacob?"

"I might be," she said while Peter shot her a speculative look.

In Peter's car Hannah started to tell him to take her to Jacob's apartment. Then suddenly she realized that wasn't where he had gone. She knew where he was and told Peter.

At the cemetery Hannah saw Jacob's car parked close to where her brother was buried. "Right here. I'll have Jacob bring me home."

Peter looked out the windshield. Although nighttime, the snow brightened the surrounding area. "Are you sure about this?"

"I'm very sure." Hannah glanced in the backseat at Andy, who had fallen asleep. "I need to make Jacob understand what it means to really forgive someone."

"Forgive?"

"I'll explain later." Hannah slid out of the car, and without peering back, walked toward the man she loved.

The next few minutes would determine the rest of her life. She firmed her resolve when Jacob lifted his head and glanced toward her. His eyes widened.

"How did you know I would be here?"

"You come every Sunday afternoon and put flowers on my brother's grave. I've known for some time."

"But this isn't Sunday afternoon."

"True. But I figured you might be here. I had Peter drop me off, so I'll need a ride home. Will you give me one?"

Nonplussed, he blinked. "Sure," he said slowly, raking his hand through his hair.

A snowflake fell, then another one.

"This is the season for hope, for new beginnings. When I came to Cimarron City, I never thought I would come face-to-face with my past, but I did. The Lord gave me a chance to right a wrong by coming here. It's not right for you to stop living because of what happened. Kevin would be the first person to tell you that. I lo—"

Jacob pressed his index finger against her lips to hush her words. "I need to say something first, Hannah. Then you can. Please?"

She nodded.

The snow increased, causing Hannah to step nearer his body's warmth. He encircled her in a loose embrace, tilting her chin up so she looked into his eyes.

"Over the years this has become the place that I come to think, to work through my problems. I feel as if I've continued my friendship with Kevin. That was important for me to believe. It kept the pain to a dull ache. Then you came into my life and made me really feel for the first time since the accident. I wanted it all—a wife, children, my life back. I just didn't know how to go about getting it."

Hope flared in her. "And you do now?"

"You were right. I have to start by forgiving myself and asking the Lord for forgiveness. That's what I've been doing."

"It's not just yourself you need to forgive but

your mother, too. What happened to you as a child has ruled your life too long. Don't let it govern your future, too."

One corner of his mouth lifted. "I'm working on that. Being around Lisa has helped me see another side to the situation. An addiction isn't easy to break. People with them need support and help, not condemnation."

She snuggled against him, seeking his warmth and nearness. "Realistic support and help. You have to know when to cut your losses, like with Nancy's mother."

"I want to be there for Lisa and Andy. I want it to work for them."

"Then we will be."

He tightened his arms about her. "I like how you use the word *we*. Hannah Collins Smith, I love you and I want to see where this relationship can go."

She chuckled. "Personally I'm hoping it leads to a house full of children, adopted and our own."

He bent his head toward hers. "I love your way of thinking."

Softly his lips grazed across hers, then took possession in a kiss that sealed an unspoken promise to love each other through the best and worst of times.

Epilogue

"This is my bedroom?" Nancy asked, standing in the doorway of a room with white furniture, a pink canopy on the bed and pink lacy curtains. "All by myself?"

Hannah entered and turned to face the seven-year-old. "Yep. Every square inch of it. What do you think?"

The little girl clapped her hands and twirled around. "I love it! I've never had my own room."

Hannah's gaze found her husband's, and a smile spread through her as she basked in the warmth of Jacob's regard. "We have a lot of bedrooms to fill."

Jacob placed his hand over Hannah's rounded stomach. "I don't think we've done too bad in a year's time. Two children and one on the way."

"Just think what we can do with a little more time," Hannah said with a laugh, thoughts of their wedding exactly a year ago producing a contentment in her that she had never thought possible until Jacob.

Terry skidded to a halt outside the bedroom and poked his head in. "Welcome to the family, Nancy."

The little girl beamed from ear to ear. "Thanks."

"Have you checked out the backyard?"

Nancy shook her head.

"C'mon. I'll show you the doghouse Jacob and I built for Abby."

As their new daughter raced after Terry, Jacob pulled Hannah back against him and ringed his arms about her. "We need to start working on the adoption papers for Gabe."

"And Susie."

His breath fanned her neck as he nibbled on her ear. "And then another of our own."

"We're gonna run out of bedrooms at this rate real quickly."

"Then we'll add on. We have the room, thanks to Peter."

Hannah swept around to face him. "Living in our own home on the ranch is the best of both worlds. I'm near my job as manager of the refuge and we have plenty of room for our children."

"Not to mention the pets they will have."

"Peter probably will never have to go out looking for homes for his animals."

"Especially with Terry as our son. With the addition of Abby we now have a cat, rabbit and two dogs."

"Just so long as we never have a snake as a pet. I draw the line at that."

"Sure, Mrs. Hartman," he murmured right before planting a kiss on her mouth. "Of course, you're going to have to tell Gabe he can't bring his garter snake with him when he comes to live with us."

She pulled back. "When did he get one?"

"He found it yesterday when Andy was visiting the refuge."

"Which reminds me, I'd better get downstairs and start lunch. Lisa and Andy should be here soon for Nancy's party. She's coming early to help me set up."

He draped his arm around her shoulder and started for the hallway. "You still don't trust me in the kitchen?"

"No, but I trust you with my heart."

* * * * *

In May 2008, be sure to pick up
FAMILY EVER AFTER, the next
installment in Margaret Daley's
FOSTERED BY LOVE miniseries.

Dear Reader,

Heart of the Family delves into a subject that is dear to my heart—our children. They are the future, and we must protect them and care for them. As a teacher, I have seen what happens when this doesn't occur. In the book I present two situations that often happen with a child in foster care. Some go back to their family and some don't. Some get adopted and some don't. Good foster parents are important to the foster-care system in this country. My thanks go out to all of them. This book is for you.

I love hearing from readers. You can contact me at P.O. Box 2074, Tulsa, OK 74101, or visit my Web site at www.margaretdaley.com where you can sign up for my quarterly newsletter.

Best wishes,

Margaret Daley

QUESTIONS FOR DISCUSSION

1. Hannah often talked to the Lord as though He were right there with her, a friend to listen to her troubles. How do you talk to the Lord? How do you pray?

2. Both Hannah and Jacob believe in Jesus, but throughout the book they must depend on their faith to make difficult decisions. How do you depend on your faith?

3. What is your favorite scene in the book? Why?

4. Jacob is tortured by something he did in his past. He can't get beyond it and forgive himself. Has anything like that happened to you or a loved one? How did you deal with it? Did you turn to the Lord?

5. Forgiveness is the cornerstone of this story. In certain situations, forgiving can be one of the hardest things you will ever do. Have you recently had to forgive someone who really hurt you? Have you ever held on to your anger and hurt because of something that was done to you? Did you pray for guidance and help? How did it make you feel when you let go of the anger and hurt?

6. Some of the children have lived rough lives in this story. How would you explain to a child that bad things happen to good people?

7. Being addicted to something can ruin a person's life because it takes over. Lisa has a hard time giving up her addiction. She realizes she can't do it alone. Have you ever dealt with an addiction or with someone who has one? What helped you to cope with it?

8. Who is your favorite character? Why?

9. What do you think is the heart of a family? Why?

10. Hannah feels the Lord has led her back to Cimarron City to help Jacob. Have you ever felt His hand in something you felt compelled to do? Have you ever felt the Lord pushed you to do something you didn't want to do? If so, how did you handle it when you were confronted with that difficult situation?

LOVE INSPIRED HISTORICAL
*Powerful, engaging stories of romance, adventure
and faith set in the past—when life was simpler
and faith played a major role in everyday lives.*

*Turn the page for a sneak preview of
HOMESPUN BRIDE by Jillian Hart
Love Inspired Historical—love and faith
throughout the ages
A brand-new line from Steeple Hill Books
Launching this February!*

There was something about the young woman—something he couldn't put his finger on. He'd hardly glanced at her when he'd hauled her from the family sleigh, but now he took a longer look through the veil of falling snow.

For a moment her silhouette, her size, and her movements all reminded him of Noelle. How about that. Noelle, his frozen heart reminded him with a painful squeeze, had been his first—and only—love.

She couldn't be here, he reasoned, since she was married and probably a mother by now. She'd be safe in town, living snugly in one of the finest houses in the county instead of riding along the country roads in a storm. Still, curiosity nibbled at him, and he plowed through the knee-deep snow. Snow was falling faster now, and yet somehow through the thick downfall his gaze seemed to find her.

She was fragile, a delicate bundle of wool—and

snow clung to her hood and scarf and cloak like a shroud, making her tough to see. She'd been just a little bit of a thing when he'd lifted her from the sleigh, and his only thought at the time had been to get both women out of danger. Now something chewed at his memory. He couldn't quite figure out what, but he could feel it in his gut.

The woman was talking on as she unwound her niece's veil. "We were tossed about dreadfully. You're likely bruised and broken from root to stem. I've never been so terrified. All I could do was pray over and over and think of you, my dear." Her words warmed with tenderness. "What a greater nightmare for you."

"We're fine. All's well that ends well," the niece insisted.

Although her voice was muffled by the thick snowfall, his step faltered. There *was* something about her voice, something familiar in the gentle resonance of her alto. Now he could see the top part of her face, due to her loosened scarf. Her eyes— they were a startling, flawless emerald green.

Whoa, there. He'd seen that perfect shade of green before—and long ago. Recognition speared though his midsection, but he already knew she was his Noelle even before the last layer of the scarf fell away from her face.

His Noelle, just as lovely and dear, was now blind and veiled with snow. His first love. The woman he'd spent years and thousands of miles trying to forget. Hard to believe that there she was suddenly right in front of him. He'd heard about the engagement announcement a few years back, and he'd known in returning to live in Angel Falls that he'd have to run into her eventually.

He just didn't figure it would be so soon and like this.

Seeing her again shouldn't make him feel as if he'd been hit in the chest with a cannonball. The shock was wearing off, he realized, the same as when you received a hard blow. First off, you were too stunned to feel it. Then the pain began to settle in, just a hint, and then rushing in until it was unbearable. Yep, that was the word to describe what was happening inside his rib cage. A pain worse than a broken bone beat through him.

Best get the sleigh righted, the horse hitched back up and the women home. But it was all he could do to turn his back as he took his mustang by the bridle. The palomino pinto gave him a snort and shook his head, sending the snow on his golden mane flying.

I know how you feel, Sunny, Thad thought. Judging by the look of things, it would be a long time until they had a chance to get in out of the cold.

He'd do best to ignore the women, especially Noelle, and to get to the work needin' to be done. He gave the sleigh a shove, but the vehicle was wedged against the snow-covered brush banking the river. Not that he'd put a lot of weight on the Lord over much these days, but Thad had to admit it was a close call. Almost eerie how he'd caught them just in time. It did seem providential. Had they gone only a few feet more, gravity would have done the trick and pulled the sleigh straight into the frigid, fast waters of Angel River and plummeted them directly over the tallest falls in the territory.

Thad squeezed his eyes shut. He couldn't stand to think of Noelle tossed into the river, fighting the powerful current along with the ice chunks. There would have been no way to have pulled her from the river in time. Had he been a few minutes slower in coming after them or if Sunny hadn't been so swift, there would have been no way to save her. To fate, to the Lord or to simple chance, he was grateful.

Some tiny measure of tenderness in his chest, like a fire long banked, sputtered to life. His tenderness for her, still there, after so much time and distance. How about that.

Since the black gelding was a tad calmer now that the sound of the train had faded off into the distance, Thad rehitched him to the sleigh but secured the driving reins to his saddle horn. He used the two horses working together to free the sleigh and get it realigned toward the road.

The older woman looked uncertain about getting back into the vehicle. With the way that black gelding of theirs was twitchy and wild-eyed, he didn't blame her. "Don't worry, ma'am, I'll see you two ladies home."

"Th-that would be very good of you, sir. I'm rather shaken up. I've half a mind to walk the entire mile home, except for my dear niece."

Noelle. He wouldn't let his heart react to her. All that mattered was doing right by her—and that was one thing that hadn't changed. He came around to help the aunt into the sleigh and after she was safely seated, turned toward Noelle. Her scarf had slid down to reveal the curve of her face, the slope of her nose and the rosebud smile of her mouth.

What had happened to her? How had she lost her sight? Sadness filled him for her blindness and for what could have been between them, once. He thought about saying something to her, so she would know who he was, but what good would that do? The past was done and over.

"Thank you so much, sir." She turned toward the sound of his step and smiled in his direction. If she, too, wondered who he was, she gave no real hint of it.

He didn't expect her to. Chances were she hardly remembered him, and if she did, she wouldn't think too well of him. She would never know what good wishes he wanted for her as he took her gloved hand. The layers of wool and leather and sheepskin lining between his hand and hers didn't stop that tiny flame of tenderness for her in his chest from growing a notch.

He looked into her eyes, into Noelle's eyes, the woman he'd loved truly so long ago, knowing she did not recognize him. Could not see him or sense him, even at heart. She smiled at him as if he were the Good Samaritan she thought he was as he helped her settle onto the seat.

Love was an odd thing, he realized as he backed away. Once, their love had been an emotion felt so strong and pure and true that he would have vowed on his very soul that nothing could tarnish or diminish their bond. But time had done that simply, easily, and they stood now as strangers.

* * * * *

*Don't miss this deeply moving
Love Inspired Historical story about a
young woman in 1883 Montana who reunites
with an old beau and soon discovers that
love is the greatest blessing of all.*

*HOMESPUN BRIDE by Jillian Hart
Available February 2008.*

*And also look for THE BRITON
by Catherine Palmer,
about a medieval lady who battles
for her family legacy—and finds true love.*

Love Inspired.
H I S T O R I C A L
INSPIRATIONAL HISTORICAL ROMANCE

THE MCKASLIN CLAN

Thad McKaslin never forgot Noelle, and her return to the Montana Territory rekindled his feelings for her. Will Noelle see how much Thad cares for her, or will her need for independence make her push him away?

LOOK FOR TWO NOVELS FROM THE NEW LOVE INSPIRED HISTORICAL SERIES EVERY MONTH.

Look for

Homespun Bride
by
JILLIAN HART

Available February 12.

Steeple
Hill®

www.SteepleHill.com

LIH82782

Love Inspired.
CLASSICS

Enjoy these four heartwarming stories
from two reader-favorite
Love Inspired authors!

2 stories in 1!

Irene Hannon
NEVER SAY GOODBYE
CROSSROADS

Lois Richer
A HOPEFUL HEART
A HOME, A HEART, A HUSBAND

These titles are available January
wherever you buy books.

Steeple
Hill®
www.SteepleHill.com

LIC0108

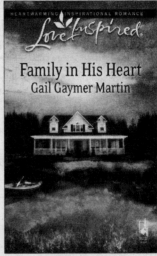

Businessman
Nick Thornton had
no misgivings about
hiring Rona Meyers, a
woman he thought was
in need of a protector.
As he got to know her,
he was humbled by her
kindness. Nick realized
maybe he was the one
in need—perhaps God
wanted him to have
a new beginning and
another chance at love.

Look for

Family in His Heart

by

Gail Gaymer Martin

Available January

wherever books are sold.

www.SteepleHill.com

Steeple
Hill®

LI87463

REQUEST YOUR FREE BOOKS!

2 FREE INSPIRATIONAL NOVELS
PLUS 2
FREE
MYSTERY GIFTS

Love Inspired®

YES! Please send me 2 FREE Love Inspired® novels and my 2 FREE mystery gifts. After receiving them, if I don't wish to receive any more books, I can return the shipping statement marked "cancel." If I don't cancel, I will receive 4 brand-new novels every month and be billed just $3.99 per book in the U.S., or $4.74 per book in Canada, plus 25¢ shipping and handling per book and applicable taxes, if any*. That's a savings of 20% off the cover price! I understand that accepting the 2 free books and gifts places me under no obligation to buy anything. I can always return a shipment and cancel at any time. Even if I never buy another book from Steeple Hill, the two free books and gifts are mine to keep forever.

113 IDN EF26 313 IDN EF27

Name	(PLEASE PRINT)	

Address		Apt. #

City	State/Prov.	Zip/Postal Code

Signature (if under 18, a parent or guardian must sign)

Order online at www.LoveInspiredBooks.com

Or mail to Steeple Hill Reader Service™:

IN U.S.A.: P.O. Box 1867, Buffalo, NY 14240-1867
IN CANADA: P.O. Box 609, Fort Erie, Ontario L2A 5X3

Not valid to current Love Inspired subscribers.

Want to try two free books from another series?
Call 1-800-873-8635 or visit www.morefreebooks.com

* Terms and prices subject to change without notice. NY residents add applicable sales tax. Canadian residents will be charged applicable provincial taxes and GST. This offer is limited to one order per household. All orders subject to approval. Credit or debit balances in a customer's account(s) may be offset by any other outstanding balance owed by or to the customer. Please allow 4 to 6 weeks for delivery.

Your Privacy: Steeple Hill is committed to protecting your privacy. Our Privacy Policy is available online at www.eHarlequin.com or upon request from the Reader Service. From time to time we make our lists of customers available to reputable firms who may have a product or service of interest to you. If you would prefer we not share your name and address, please check here. ☐

LIREG07

Love Inspired®
SUSPENSE
RIVETING INSPIRATIONAL ROMANCE

A thug attempted to abduct Julia Daniels at gunpoint in broad daylight. And whoever was after the widowed mother would stop at nothing, including shooting a police officer. Handsome deputy sheriff Eric Butler was on the case, but he needed the truth about who she was running from. Yet how could Julia tell him when it meant putting all their lives in grave danger?

Look for
Deadly Texas Rose
by LENORA WORTH

Available January wherever books are sold.

Steeple
Hill®

www.SteepleHill.com

LIS44275

TITLES AVAILABLE NEXT MONTH

Don't miss these four stories in January

FAMILY IN HIS HEART by Gail Gaymer Martin
Nick Thornton could tell Rona Meyers was a special person, so he'd offered her a much-needed job. And as he got to know her, he couldn't stop wondering if God was offering him a new beginning and a second chance at love.

NEXT DOOR DADDY by Debra Clopton
A Mule Hollow novel

When rancher Nate Talbert prayed for a change to his reclusive life, he got new next-door neighbor Pollyanna McDonald. But the menagerie of pets that she and her son cared for was driving him *crazy*. Could he handle the chaos that surrounded her?

THE DOCTOR'S BRIDE by Patt Marr
Everyone in town was trying to find Dr. Zack Hemingway a wife. Yet the one girl who caught his eye wasn't interested. Why was Chloe Kilgannon hiding from him? This doctor knew it would take some good medicine to get to the heart of the matter.

A SOLDIER'S PROMISE by Cheryl Wyatt
Wings of Refuge

Pararescue jumper Joel Montgomery had the power to make a sick little boy's dream come true. He was determined to follow through even if it meant returning to a place he'd rather forget. And meeting the boy's pretty teacher made his leap of faith doubly worth the price.

LICNM1207